With The Eleven

This book is a work of fiction. Any resemblance to actual events or persons, living or dead, is entirely coincidental.

"With the Eleven," by Robert Jeffrey Grant. ISBN 1-58939-846-7.

Published 2006 by Virtualbookworm.com Publishing Inc., P.O. Box 9949, College Station, TX 77842, US. ©2006, Robert Jeffrey Grant. All rights reserved. No part of this publication may be reproduced, stored in a retrieval system, or transmitted in any form or by any means, electronic, mechanical, recording or otherwise, without the prior written permission of Robert Jeffrey Grant.

Manufactured in the United States of America.

With the Eleven

by
Robert Jeffrey Grant

Table of Contents

1 - Gin Milling 1

2 - Trapped Five-O 43

3 - Cold French Fries 65

4 - Nomad Monks 93

5 - Today go workah-Tomorrow go workah .. 109

6 - Boat Won't Work 123

7 - Fire Extinguishers 155

8 - Road Trip 175

9 - S FL Telemarketers 205

10 - Hurricane Warning 221

11 - A Dollar's Value 246

1 - Gin Milling

"I need to buy a car. It's going to rain out. Look at those clouds--clouds big and dark and KABOOM!" Franky's voice carried to Ray's ears, the latter being eighty four with hearing as sharp as a German Shepherd's. The two men being the same age, and northerners as well. Larry from Jersey, Ray from New York and I from Providence RI. We all felt at ease with one another at the dog track.

Ray pivoted on his stool, "A car, a car--I gotta buy a car," he imitated Larry in an over exasperated thin, week, comic groan. "Gimme a break, "Ray's voice rose even sharper and louder so it carried as far as Mike the program man, located more than halfway on the other side of the large first floor, could easily hear. "You say that every

2

week. You have plenty of money--what the hell," Ray turned to me.

Franky piped up, "Yeah, I know, I think I'll buy one."

"Yeah sure. Sure. I hear this every day. He tells me this every day, "Ray turned to me. "His car it isn't even covered. You're foolish Franky not to have a car, with the damn cover--that's ripped; it don't even cover you. I seen you come in here all wet. Geez," Ray moaned then whirled as he heard the turnstile. A young thug and his girlfriend entered the track and were speeding away from Ray toward the program stand.

"Ahh Geez--Damnit! You owe me a dollar!" he boomed as spit shot out of his mouth.

The girl turned around. The guy kept going. This was such a common tandem occurrence although it was a newcomer, but so often I'd witnessed the same thing; the guy oblivious with headphones on would carelessly bounce to the program stand while the girlfriend would turn and pull on the young hood's arm. I was curious to see how Ray would handle this one. Sometimes he'd keep screaming at them to 'get back here--you owe me a dollar!' Or he'd say to the girl with disgust, 'Go ahead...go ahead,' before the boyfriend ever became wise to his own err, which warranted a tug on his arm by his bitch; a major problem interrupting his rap tune I garnered from his irksome face. Other times, Ray would say, 'You went through the wrong turnstile. Now I've gotta get up and turn it. Attendance has to match the money.' Some people would come back and turn it for the old man, which earned points with Ray, or, at least settled him down. If not, I'd hear him complain about the young peoples' lack of manners for around twenty minutes.

"It's not like it was up north. In those days, we had class. Even if we were being obnoxious at least we paid attention to what was going on around us. These jadrules are all out in left field. I think the girlfriends are the only ones with an ounce of sense left. I used to come into the Tracks even up north like I was some type of big shot. I didn't care. I'd buy broads--did all of that shit--spent money. I was a big-time ballplayer.

"What sport?"

"Basketball. I played for Toronto."

"When?"

"Ah. A long time ago, I played in the first NBA game vs. Cleveland. Used to play in the

Garden."

"The Boston Garden?"

"Sure. But I'm talking about Madison Square Garden."

"You played for the New York Knicks too?"

"No. During my college days, I played for St. John's. I used to think I was a big shot. I was only a freshman. I didn't know who I thought I was. But one day, I told the coach...I had the balls to say...'Coach, I'm not going to play tonight unless my friends,' who I'd met at a local gin mill, 'unless my friends can play instead of the school band.' Well, he thought about it and I thought he was going to tell me to go to hell or somewhere. But he says, 'Okay Ray.' And they played."

Ray's eyes became very warm and lost the sharpness from the ire the youngsters drew out of him. Memory lane was a place I could tell he enjoyed to be. I'd listen to him reminisce with Lefty about the old glory days at the track down here in South Florida.

"When the parking lots were full," Lefty said to me, as Ray looked on proudly, "people used to dress up to come here--Here! Can you believe it?" Lefty threw his arms up. "Lots of changes, huh Ray?"

"Ppff--Sure."

"Did this guy tell you about all the bars he owned? Or the woman he dated? He owned three gin mills and dated that actress?"

"That's right. And I was married six times."

Lefty laughed as my eyebrows arched.

"I miss it. There's no more..." Ray bent his knees and thrust his hips forward while pulling his arms backward by his hips.

"You must," Lefty winked at me.

"Ah oh Ray," Ray said to himself, "You're a PIP Ray--a real PIP, ah well."

Just then old Vince walked by.

"Hey Nate!" Ray thundered.

The ninety year old short man with black glasses turned and waved.

"That guy--I'll tell you, he's funny. He got a blowjob a couple months ago."

"Really?" I said.

"Sure. He gives me hope. At ninety and still doing that, geez. I haven't..."

I interrupted, "Tell me about the gin mill you owned."

"Well, I'll tell ya! My relief is here so I need to count the money. Good. We balance. I thought that kid through me off earlier, but I'm okay."

Ray stooped over as he put on his Miami Heat hat and smiled at me.

"All right champ. I'm going to go watch the Heat and have a nice glass of scotch or two--and maybe see the broad upstairs. She's a little wacky so I don't know."

Picture Book of Memories

Ray relayed his night to me, answering my inquiry.

"Well, I went home, yelled at the refs on the T.V. as the Heat lost--those bums. I could show'em a lesson or two. He feigned a jump shot. Then I called that girl. I think we'll take a trip to Vegas. I got married there once, no twice. Shit, I've been married in many of our big cities once--but there twice."

I laughed. "Why Vegas?"

He replied, "I used to live there. A lot of these guys did. I go back once every couple of years. I play Craps; that's the only game for me."

"I like Blackjack."

His eyes lit up like a turned on slot. "Well sure." Ray had a wonderful way of saying that loud, exuberant, yet reassuring as if it was to be expected that was the game of choice for me.

"You can make a lot of money in that game too. I win big at the beginning, but I give most of it back."

"Like everyone?"

"Sure--what the hell. You're there to have fun. I don't give a damn."

A gangly patron came in. "Hey Ray."

"Hey Babe."

The patron announced, "I've got a hefty price tag on this week's lobster catch. I'll treat you at the horse track. You guys going Saturday?"

"Sure. I'm going. I'll be there."

The man turned his back. And Ray took the opportunity to say,

"Ahh, you're full of shit ya," he said to the man's back, but loud enough that he may've heard Ray.

Now Ray addressed me. "He tells me he has a great catch of lobsters or fish every week and tells me he'll treat. I'm the one ends up paying for his beer."

Then something happened that made me

forget that I had no friends in South Florida yet, aside from Ray being my sole buddy.

Ray walked in. He placed his newspaper under his coat. I started to review the dream I had. It was Johnny Lang singing in what seemed like an outdoor concert, but it was dark out. There were streaks, long streaks of light on his face. His visage came close to me, or more accurately, the lens of my mind's eye moved to a close-up of him. The blues singer appeared handsomer in the dream. As the song ended, there were Cirque De Soleil dancers--bright orange and white and hot pink boas flailed freely around their tanned necks, as Tahitian women. A strange finale to a blues concert, I thought, when Ray jarred my thoughts with, "One hundred thirty."

"What?" I said.

He pointed at the last of the cars on the train that steamed north.

"I counted them. They have sand in the back of them. I don't know which beaches they take them from or to...maybe they take them to the desert for all I know."

"You counted them?"

"Sure."

Ray opened the paper. It wasn't a newspaper after all, but a gaming paper as I could see the bold, black ODDS heading concerning several baseball games.

"I never learned how to bet on baseball, I explained, "but I used to bet football in high school and college."

Ray explained, "Well, that's the only one I didn't bet on because my dad used to play professionally and he didn't want me betting on baseball so I didn't. But I had a friend who made a living doing it. He'd bet on streaks. Historically, and it holds true today, that a team, particularly favorites on good teams will go on long streaks. Bet to win until they lose and vice versa."

"That works?"

"Sure. He made a killing--one of the richest guys I ever met and I've met a lot of high rollers."

The money intrigued me as my agents, when they paid me were often late and the checks for extra work were anything but. I needed the money. The track didn't give me any overtime. But gambling was never my forte nor was I blessed with luck in any aspect of my life. I wasn't about to start with baseball of all sports, where one lucky swing with the bases loaded could be your undoing. I peeked at the ads with scantily clad girls littered between the odds papers and story contents.

"I booked a place for me and that girl in my building at this hotel. I tried to envision Ray there--his playboy days well behind him and what the girl from his apartment looked like and how they would look in one of the Desert's brightly lit hotels.

"You want to go?" Ray asked me, "The broad canceled."

"Oh no I can't. I mean I should stay here."

"Why? You have some vacation time," Ray persisted.

"But it's off season in Vegas now, isn't it? I'd rather go in season."

"There's no off season in Vegas. It's Vegas," Fritz shrugged with a coy grin. "Why don't you go with him?" Fritz offered.

"No I can't."

"Aw geez." Ray laughed and Fritz' laughter was such an infectious underbelly to Ray that I relented.

"So it is--it's Vegas. I'm all in," I feigned pushing chips across the table and clasped hands with Ray to their delight.

We drank Scotch on the plane. And on the flight Ray and I became fast friends. I tried my best to keep track of his ex-wives.

"The third one was okay," he informed. "But I was running around too much and she didn't want to put up with the actresses I was dating on the side. She was religious and I wasn't. All the rest of my wives were floosies compared to her. Some days I think what if I stayed."

"Why didn't you?"

"You can't teach an old dog new tricks. I'm a son of a bitch I tell ya. She never used to bitch and moan like the rest of them though. I give her credit for that. The only time she got mad, well I knew she was mad. But she begged me all the time about our wedding day."

"What happened?" I braced myself though I knew the Scotch had loosened me up to where I was bold enough to dare personal questions. I wasn't so sure if the Scotch had settled into the old Polark's veins.

Ray didn't glance up from his Scotch or twitch in any disconcerted manner.

He continued, "I made her get married in Vegas."

"So?"

"She was religious and wanted to get married in a church. I pushed for one of the overnight chapels in Vegas so I could get back to the craps table or whatever else I was doing at the time. Her family never forgave me and I don't think she ever did really either."

"Well, it's not so easy to forgive especially those that we're close to."

"Naw. I don't blame her. Either way, I've learned to live and let the chips fall where they may."

He held his hands up high, spread apart and feathered out his fingers as he lowered his skinny arms. I followed them down to his face, which wore a big smile serving to instantly change our somber mood. "It's Vegas Babe. Let's play!" say Ray.

We milled around the casino floor for a gander of the sights, lights, and drink. After a couple rounds, I looked behind her and picked out a bottle hiding in the back. Its shape intrigued me. It seemed of a different age.

"Ray, do you mind if we switch gears here and try some of that up there?"

"Sure. What type of Scotch is it?" he squinted as he leaned to the left almost rubbing shoulders with me.

"It's gin." The bartender placed the bottle in front of Ray. "Very old--my owner said never to open it. The bartender then read the label on the bottle and repeated its slogan as if he were reciting words to a play,

'The Sun Never Sets on Gilbey's Gin.'

"I'll be damned," Ray said in awe.

"You've had it before?" asked the bartender.

"Sure. My distributor used to stock this for me at the gin mills I operated, especially the last one."

I couldn't decipher if the bottle brought back good memories or bad.

Ray's thumbs lined each concave side above the bottles base, jutting slightly upward at the shoulders. One could rest a nickel in each side because of the cupping angles of the antiquated bottle, which was in remarkably good shape. He then traced the gold and white diamond label then looked under the bottom gold label where the distributor print read, 'Cincinnati.'

"Cincinnati," said Ray aloud, "that's where the driver would come up from every Thursday around noon. I'd tell him to park the truck behind my car around back, before the joint got hoppin' around happy hour. He loved my car."

"What was it?" asked the bartender.

"A Hudson Commodore--two toned. It was unmatched by any other stock car. That was their slogan too, and that's why I bought it. What the hell, I was a big-shot back then. Anyways, after this guy...Henry, that was his name, Henry after he finished stocking the gin how I wanted it and everything, he used to play a polka on my Wurlitzer jukebox. You should've seen him dance."

"He danced alone?"

"Naw, they'd usually be a few girls in even that early in my joint. It was like they never left. Yup." Ray lowered his eyes to read again, "The Sun Never Sets on Gilbeys Gin. That's true--especially if my bartender Tommy worked. Boy, did he like to party."

"Where was your bar?"

"New York."

"My boss is from there. His name is

Tommy too."

"Tommy what?"

"Tommy Bushell."

"Oh Christ," Ray clapped his hands together. "He's out here at this place. We'll have to come by and pay him a visit. Tell him Ray Wertis stopped by."

"You're Ray Wertis? You played for Toronto."

"Sure."

"Well, Mr. Bushell, he used to talk a lot about you. I'm sure he wouldn't mind if I served you guys a drink from his Gilbey's Gin bottle."

"Naw. That's all right."

"Why not?" the bartender asked.

I wondered this myself and secretly hoped that Ray would change his mind. The bottle seemed to have a mesmerizing power.

"I don't mix. I'm a Scotch man now."

The man stared at him and paused before he grabbed the bottle and placed it behind the others. It leaned outward like the Eiffel Tower; the view if one was sitting in my seat. Ray filled the bartender in on some glory year's stories. I laughed and listened along though I glanced at the bottle whenever there were any pauses in their conversation.

The parts of their conversations that interested me were twofold: certainly the baseball theme as well as the history of New York to a degree.

I tuned in to Ray relaying a baseball tidbit to the bartender.

"Johnny Price at Ebbets Filed, one game, liked to pitch while standing on his head. He was entertaining so my dad would buy tickets whenever the Indians came into town; or he'd pick the tix up from the front office was more like it. Yeah, a lot of good times. The year all us Dodger fans in a darkened Ebbets Field, must have been 33,000 of us holding lit matches as part of a tribute to team captain Pee Wee Reese in 1955. I used to smoke enough for a whole section of people so it wasn't nothing to me, chomping on my cigar all night like I always did. It was the Little Colonel's (Reese's nickname also) 36th birthday."

"How long was his career?" I asked.

"He was slotted at shortstop since 1940 with the exception of a few years during World War II. On game days, my mom and I would take the nickel fare subways."

"A nickel! Damn--you must've loved that," the bartender echoed.

"Sure. In those days, before he started making better money in the major leagues, we'd get around like the rest of New Yorkers. It was a golden age for us subway passengers; we had no car for quite some time. The subway enabled millions of New Yorkers to take full advantage of the cities' sights, to attend inexpensive concerts at Town Hall, where I met my first wife, or visit City College, where I met my second wife, to WPA jobs, which was where I met my third wife; I told you plenty about her on the plane. Or the train could take you to the western side of the Hudson, where hundreds of miles of railroad tracks could be found," he smiled here. "The tracks ran from new Jersey, Hoboken and smaller towns. She took me. I was just a tiny tot, but I remember her paying a nickel from her purse, hearing it prattle around by the conductor.

Boy, I remember your boss, Tommy Bushell, telling me about hard times. His dad went out of business during the abolishment of the pushcarts in 1930. Getting in the bar business was a smart move. It wasn't easy, but eventually he came across some influentials in the Port Authority. See, by 1928 to 1939, the Great Depression crushed The Interborough and The Brooklyn Manhattan; the rapid transit traffic of the BMT declined by 23%. Then by the early 1930's, the survival of The Interborough and The Brooklyn Manhattan as private companies, along with the physical integrity of the subway system itself was in jeopardy.

But then, in 1921, The Port Authority, with New York and New Jersey, started to gain financial strength due to its control of the Holland Tunnel revenues. Paul Windel, instrumental in all this, indirectly was responsible for giving your boss's dad his gin mill and me too further down the line, he was. Ironically, the Transit Authority was established just in time to preside over the subway's decline."

Ray dropped his head. "Though that Windel, an investor, helped build my gin mills up...I miss those days of the nickel fares. He reached in his pocket. Bring that bottle back down."

When the bartender placed it in front of him, Ray balanced a nickel on each side of the Gin bottle.

"Are you positive you don't want a

slug?" asked the seller.

Ray shook his head.

I was bummed so asked, "What happened to your gin mills Ray?"

The bartender waved his hand and cringed as if that was a common knowledge topic to avoid at all costs.

After a torturous silence, Ray turned red for the first time and reached for his wallet, "Give us a double…Scotch."

I felt like knowing and sorry to have insulted Ray, tried to think of something to say to get off the subject.

"When did Brooklyn win their first championship?"

That seemed to do the trick for the redness drained out of him as well as his withering frame became lively again.

"Jackie Robinson used to taunt pitchers with animated leadoffs," Ray began. "And in 1955 he stole home in the World Series under a pitch from Whitey Ford to Yogi Berra, to help Brooklyn win the first game of the series and ultimately, their first World Championship. We had seats right behind the plate."

I note that the nickels stayed put all night into the wee hours.

Ray and Almost Famous in Vegas

The ads for jobs were depressing. I didn't want to be a waiter. Masseuse sounded like a good option but Ray was right. What if you got some Bubatsa with rolls of fat? ... No. I wondered how much money Ray had. We both decided to call it quits from Florida and give Vegas a shot after all.

I could stay out late in the casinos and know that Ray wouldn't gripe about my not working. And I was winning at my game, Blackjack, anyhow. I kept track of the amount I won, day by day. And week by week. Time flew by, but I wouldn't really know in the clockless time of Sin City. Shows merged into shows, bets into bets, and broads into broads. I don't know what made me pick up the paper to look in the classifieds in the first place. Sit back and enjoy this ride. And I did...until one night something made me think long and hard.

The night in question, which I think it was a weekend night, or maybe Thursday evening, and is basically the same thing for anyone visiting or living in Las Vegas. Anyhow, we were paying a visit to the bartender with the nickels atop the leaning gin.

"Haven't seen you guys in over a month," remarked the barkeep.

Ray and I discussed how busy we'd been cleaning out the casinos. He, with his craps game and me with Blackjack, when Ray barked, "You're boss--he used to like Craps. Give me that nickel."

The bartender pulled the one off the Gin bottle that looked as if it would fall anyway.

"Last year in Vegas a guy was playing Craps and was a mangy looking guy, but he left the table with four grand in less than a half hour--smart guy. I was watching him the whole time. He started with nickels. They call those five dollar bets," Ray informed me of the terminology. "And he worked his way up smartly to quarter bets, $25.00," he expressively raised his eyebrows to clarify his gaming references and made sure I was on the same page as he.

As Ray embellished slightly, our glorious streak of gambling, I fantasized about the lifestyle that I never had. Sexy broads draped on your arm as you made cool bet after cool bet--and they'd bring the head all night into the wee hours.

We had our winnings and our women, but it wasn't four grand in a half hour nor were they the women of the eye-popping variety that we'd pass in all the casinos especially by the high roller tables. I saw how the people treated Ray with respect. He had connections out here. But he'd experienced the high life already, years ago. I hadn't. He'd led. And he had the easy manner of a leader. I hadn't and didn't. But I wanted to.

Soon after racking my brain how, I finally tuned back into the conversation where Ray pondered, "Ah. Those were good times."

Where in memory lane this time, I wondered. Ebbets field, helping the FBI in one of the many Miami murder cases Ray had investigated, a sting operation perhaps.

Ray commiserated in rhetoric only with the bartender, which relieved me. "How's the craic? You know…that old Irish slang to describe the atmosphere of a good pub, including the food, the drink, music, even down to the conversation."

"How was the craic in your gin mill Ray?" asked the barkeep.

I didn't expect the poignancy of the bartender's question. I braced myself for a look or a thunderous, 'mind your own business!' But Ray answered calmly,

"From the moment the patrons signed 'The Book'--that is a registry of daily patrons," Ray turned to enlighten me. "Each day the regulars signed the book and would throw a dollar in the monthly pool. At the end of the month, I'd pick a name out of a hat. And that person was drawn to win the jackpot--a sizeable jackpot."

I smiled. I loved the way he emphasized the word sizeable.

"What would the winner spend the money on?" asked the bartender.

Ray smoothed the table and grinned with a snicker. "That's the best part babe," his mouth opening and body beginning to shake with joyous life--they'd usually end up spending it right thee at my gin mill. Geez. Some nights they'd even purchase countless rounds of Orange Blossoms, My Place or No Place, Lady Scarlett's, Kiss Offs. You name it."

He continued, "Ah--it was beautiful," he sighed happily with eyes gazing up over the barkeep and beyond the back of the leaning bottle of gin.

My eyes followed his and stayed there, pinned to the last remaining nickel on the right side of the bottle, higher up then the left, but inactive. That's me, I thought--inactive, as Ray twirled the nickel in his fingers, listening to the bartender tell him about a large pub with a small casino for sale down the strip just a stone's throw from here.

"Why don't we buy the place Ray?"

"Not enough money from what the bartender tells me."

"How short are we?"

"We're a long way short--let me tell you. And even if we were long I'd be hesitant to jump back on the gin mill bandwagon. You'd have better luck getting this old fart up on those fucking treadmills these exercise fanatics do in their fancy gyms." He laughed.

I still wanted to know what soured him on gin mills, but said,

"What if I came up with 75% of the money? Would you invest the rest then?"

"Sure. I'd be a silent partner--what the hell."

"I'd need you to give me advice though so don't be too silent."

"I've never been known to be--for long."

I used Ray's friend's strategy for betting on baseball. And it worked month after month. I collected thousands upon thousands of dollars. I kept this quiet from Ray. He knew I was winning, just not how much. The only thing that made me more nervous than anticipating when a team's streak was turning one way or another, was the petrifying perusing of the real estate page to check that our prospective gin mill hadn't been sold. When the playoffs started, I saw a for sale sign. I called the realtor who said it looked as if the buyer was about to change his mind. This seesaw even continued into October and the World Series. After the Marlins won their fourth game, I partied hard and rejoiced to know it was still for sale. Now I just had to approach Ray. But before I could muster up the courage, I needed to go see that bottle of gin and the nickel.

"What do you know about Ray's gin mills? Why did he lose them?" I blurted out to the bartender immediately upon my purposeful arrival.

"They were taken from him--gambling debts. One day some hooded men came in and said, 'Payment is due super ballplayer.' Ray reached for his gun. But his old lady screamed no. And he hesitated. Ray was a great shot. For as good a shooter he was in the NBA he was even better with a pistol. You could ask anyone on the Miami P.D. says my boss. Well, the three guys had him dead to rights--all pointing a pistol at him. Ray put his gun down and said, 'I don't have it fellas. You can have my other two places.' But it wasn't enough. They demanded his first gin mill--the one where his dad spent the first nickel in the place. It was embedded, framed by Ray into the wall. 'Okay, give me til tomorrow,' Ray pleaded. 'No,' the guy says, 'when the sun sets tonight I want you outta here and I better never see you again.' Ray was pissed because he wanted to get the nickel out, but the sun was to set in a half hour--enough time to clear out his licker and drink a bottle of gin.

'The Sun Never Sets' ... "on Gilbey's Gin," I added.

"Yup. That was his last drink in one of his

gin mills."

"What happened to the nickel?"

"No one knows. The place burned down in 1979. Ray always regrets not having gone back to get it, my boss said."

"What about the wife?"

"The wife...the wife lost respect for him. They actually got in a heated argument. Ray blamed her, for if she hadn't screamed, 'no,' that he'd have blown the robbers' hoods off. Instead old Ray got behind the hood of his Commodore and drove us far south as it took him. He didn't stop til he landed at a little inn by one of the casino boats in South Florida. He joined the force that year and had a legendary career at the Miami P.D. as you are aware of."

"I really want to run a casino with him. You think he'll give me his 25%?"

"I don't think he wants to get involved in gaming, or gin milling again."

"Why? Shit--that's practically all he discusses?

"It's his persona. He likes to drag around those past glory days. We all do naturally."

"Right. That's all I want now--my share of glory."

But listen, Ray worked hard--and he lost

out. I'm sure he don't want you to get hurt in this shady business. Plus, those hoods might still be alive. If he's on the books, say at your new place should you purchase it, sooner or later they might come looking for him."

"Why?"

"In Miami in the '60's old Ray pinched two of those New York gin mill triggermen, identified them with his own eyes. The third guy was in L.A. Ray looks for him out here in Vegas every year--says he'll get the bastard and make him show him where the nickel is."

"Why didn't Ray ever tell me this?"

"He can't--not without crying. And Ray, he don't cry. Ever."

I asked Ray for the money. He posed a challenge to me.

"If you can win more money at Craps than me this weekend than sure I'll do it."

"That's unfair. I've never played Craps before. Blackjack?

"Craps or nothing."

"Shit. I had to learn the game.

I watched some players play it. The table was intimidating--the size of a pool table and as comfortable, as Ray felt playing pool and betting on the pool size Craps table, I felt as uncomfortable. I was used to Blackjack a half a sphere table where I could see the action at a glance and the kind cards with faces. The die, whether red or white, with the 'take a number philosophy' didn't register with my brain. Plus, there were too many people from the casino working there. The two side dealers, the bayman, the switzer, floor man, pit boss, too many gaming options--come bets, right bettor, wrong bettor, single odds, double odds. With Blackjack, there was only the dealer and double down. I looked and listened to the dealers' conversations, and only took away this, George means a good tipper or toker, and Tome means a bad toker. They counted their money and I wondered how I'd ever beat Ray at his own game.

I went to church--Saint Joseph's. I felt like I needed the patron saint of bettors, but the patron saint of houses would do cuz I needed to beat the house in a sense, using the casino's chips, nickels and quarters in Ray's own words, before I could surpass Ray and get his 25% and ultimately my piece on the strip.

30

As I knelt down, I hurriedly blessed myself in the darkness. I gazed at the small candle-lit bulbs, 5 tiers deep, maybe 12 across. I could flick them on, but opted to pray in darkness for the grace to beat Ray. After a few moments, I raised my head and noticed a ring atop the thin rusty colored, bronze natalier cross which held court steadily below the tray of bulbs, many of which were unlit. I slid the ring off the cross; the dust from the ring nearly made me sneeze as I stuck it in my pocket.

It had been so dark and depressing in the church. As I turned the corner to the strips layered succession of lights, I felt a hand on my shoulder.

"Hi," a female voice said. "Don't be startled. I saw you in the church. Are you part of the faithful?" she inquired with bright eyes.

"No," I stammered, looking down. I just need something."

"Oh--I hope your wish is granted."

"What is your name?"

"A.F."

"My name is Yvonne. I teach yoga. We

don't have many regulars. I am praying for customers. Will you come to a session?"

"I don't know. I'm kind of busy."

"Well, if you decide to come, here is the address."

I folded the card into my wallet and watched her gold and token colored hair, filled with tussles, bounce fully down the street into the darkness as I shielded my eyes from the Strip's bright lights.

"Ray--have a hot date tonight I see."

"Yup. We're going to a show. Want to come? This is Andrea."

I shook her hand.

"He's A.F.--going to be a movie star some day."

Ray stepped into the cab.

"Casino owner!" I substituted as he followed the girl, sliding in beside her. I saw his profile smile briefly.

I lost mightily to Ray. Yvonne comforted me. She said my attendance wasn't enough to keep her business afloat so she moved to Los Angeles.

Months went by. She called one Sunday and said she'd hooked into doing some producing now as well as a side gig in a yoga studio with plenty of customers. I convinced Ray to go out to L.A. with me for the weekend. He agreed, said it was the least he could do in light of the thrashing he laid on me in Craps. I couldn't have felt more the same way.

L'il Rich Poodle

A clothed poodle crossed the street. Ray, after a long pause with saucer-like eyes that gaped as if the pouch was indeed a person, exclaimed, "Look at that fucking thing-- dressed up like she's going out for a night on the town. Geez." He laughed his wheezy, inhaling laugh, which lifted his shoulders on the inhale then drooped on the exhale.

"Where is this shoot located anyhow?" his impatience emerging.

"It's in my instructors backyard."

"Backyard? Couldn't they afford studio

time? The cheapskates."

"You won't say that when you see this place. It's chic."

"Sure. It better be, in a neighborhood like this one."

Ray lit a cigar and looked like he should be at a dog track not to be heading behind the scenes at a movie shoot.

"I hope you finish that before we get to the producer's house," I warned.

"Judging by how long we've been walking, I'd have time to smoke another one."

We arrived and Ray pulled up a chaise lounge on the high courtyard aloft by the producer's mansion.

"Guess this is nice," Ray said looking at the Mexican cameraman set up a tripod.

I nodded, still looking down at the waterfall, which led to a small rivulet stocked with coy; they could swim to either side of the larger lagoon.

"Help yourself to the food," said the producer.

There were grapes, cheeses, and juices and muffins to snack on. I tried to gauge their reactions to Ray. He looked as if he didn't fit in, dipping his cheese into the dip, but I felt nervous. There were six other people to read lines before me. I was glad Ray was here. He'd keep me loose, or at least looser than I'd be on my own.

Ray watched the first few men auditioning with interest. He told me how he showed up on the set with an actress he dated in the old days, "But it was in New York. This is nicer. God--look at that pool."

The producer's assistant overheard him, "Would you like to go in?" she asked.

"Naw--I'm just here to make sure my friend here gets the starring role."

I was grateful. But as the next man auditioned, I was looking at Ray sweat and felt he may be at risk for heat stroke. There was only this guy then me. My nerves oughta be okay from here on, I reasoned.

"Why don't you go in?"

"I don't have a suit. These knickers weren't much, but they are my best pair."

"There's all sizes upstairs. Try one on," the assistant urged.

"Go ahead," I concurred.

"All right. It's a little hot. Good luck A.F.--knock'em dead."

"It's upstairs, last room on the left," the assistant gave Ray directions.

We watched him slowly make his way into the mansion's back entrance.

"Man, such a beautiful house," I complimented.

"Yes. We are lucky to shoot here. They usually don't give access to the setting."

"I thought you own the place."

"Just a smaller house down the lane--it's on the property but.... One of the studio heads owns it."

"Is he here?"

"No."

Ray made his way into the pool, which was beneath the courtyard toward the street, and was concealed by tall thick bushes. I watched a cabana boy pour him some grapefruit juice from a glass pitcher. I reviewed my lines a last time.

Yvonne approached me saying, "I'm so glad you took up yoga. This is where your dream becomes a reality. It's okay you didn't get the casino, you know. For this reason something bigger, better…this role."

"I suppose you are right. I wonder what would've happened if I had beaten Ray."

"Don't think about it. You need to get this part. Nail it shut sweetie," she leaned toward me on the white chaise lounge and hooked my arm in hers and rubbed my bicep. It felt so smooth and sexy yet hard. She smiled her beautiful Panama smile at me. I was stunned how beautiful she was, how beautiful this place was, how lucky I was to begin a relationship with a yoga teacher who also was assistant to perhaps the biggest Hollywood producer.

I watched her ass wiggle away; and on the pear-shaped derriere a blue imprinted 'yoga' boldly swayed advertising, while slightly gripping snugly around the delicate bottom of her long white pants.

Ray heard a car pull up; ears attuned to a jingle, which became nearer, possibly a dog. It now sounded clear enough to guess it may be the white poodle he and A.F. had seen earlier. Ray pressed his hand against the top step of the concrete and rose gingerly from the pool's second. He stood on tiptoes and stared at the dog. A man whistled and the dog turned hastily to follow him up toward the side-front entrance, it appeared to Ray. He felt badly, making fun of the dog earlier. It probably belonged to one of the heavies in the studio and he didn't want any bad vibes affecting A.F.'s audition.

37

The man noticed Ray's trunks draped over the shower. From his back pocket, the man flipped a comb into his hand and returned to his poodle which he began brushing.

I watched the tape on the laptop's monitor. The competition could be whittled to three, Yvonne surmised though the she wouldn't settle the audition in question. I was a finalist at this point. But was she truly objectionable or had our past relationship taint her bias? I'd have to wait. Luckily, the studio gave us access to the grounds for the afternoon.

"We should know by sundown, Yvonne apprised me. "You want to use the spa? Get a masseuse?"

"Maybe I'll join Ray in the pool--unless I could pry you away from that laptop and join me."

"I don't know. We'll see. Angelino is home now. He just beeped me so he will want my input on the decision--so that is good for you. My massage can wait, no?"

"Who is that by the pool?" Angelino asked Yvonne,

"A.F.'s friend, Raymond."

"I have seen him before...in Las Vegas, yes. He looks like he's frightfully searching for something always."

"He's just curious. An old man in a new neighborhood. Relax. Here, I'll give you a shiatsu massage. I know you're shoulder is sore. Come lie your face on the bed."

Yvonne returned to me.

"Did you finish? Did Angelino decide?"

"No. I gave him a quick massage. Now I need one," she stretched on the table.

"Gladly." I began massaging her--she gasped where I placed the hot stones.

Angelino went down to the courtyard.

"Where is Yvonne?" he asked a production assistant.

"I don't know. We thought you were reviewing it with her."

"No. I needed work on my shoulder first. Where's A.F.?"

"Probably in the house."

Ray toweled off by the pool and spied Angelino. That was him--the hooded man! This wasn't how he envisioned it. He wanted that nickel. He thought of the rage and shame this man had caused him, failed marriages, three gin mills; and now he was here with the power to make or break A.F.'s dreams. Should he be polite and back off? Ray knew that if he could get upstairs where his gun was draped over the sink in his gray and blue knickers that he would feel that itch that he'd felt and this time there'd be no wife to tell him, 'no.' He could blaze away all the brewed anger and hatred that this man had shaken and stirred in him for so long and after he'd feel peace. He knew that much.

But A.F.--he thought how disappointed A.F. was that the casino sold and that he, Ray, had held out on him. He couldn't risk it for A.F.'s sake at this juncture. But what if old Angelino recognized him? If so then it'd surely be worth killing the now overweight slob. He got up and walked calmly by

Angelino who was starting the elimination process. Ray watched the man's eyes intent on the laptop. Yes. No doubt, thought Ray, those green eyes with turquoise waves in them were ones that he could never forget.

"Old man if you're going in the house, call Yvonne. Will you please?"

Ray nodded affirmatively to Angelino's request.

The poodle barked and Yvonne grabbed the stones off her own body. I better go to the bedroom. Angelino is getting restless I'm sure, she reminded herself. She walked into the bedroom.

After putting on his knickers, Ray fingered the gun and stared out the window. He drew it out and fired. Yvonne burst through the door and screamed. She peered out the window to see Angelino slumped onto his laptop. She ran out of the room by where I was and I raced after her. She sobbed and cradled her husband. I watched myself on the laptop say my last lines, which weren't needed, for Angelino had scribbled on a piece of paper, 'Leading man role--A.F.'

A voice with humility said, "Sorry. I couldn't help it."

Ray continued, "I tried to calm myself down when I knew it was him, but I go from A-Z. I've always been that way. He stole my gin mills ruined my life. My wife--she had no respect for me--Gladys."

"Gladys," I repeated, "that was her name?" Though he'd told me much about her, I realized he'd never referred to her by name before this moment.

Ray nodded sadly.

I pulled out a ring. "Could this be yours?"

It was the ring I'd found in St. Joseph's. He read the inscription, "Gladys, I'm home."

He tossed it in the pool, walked after it. His back toward us. His directions turned aimlessly for his next few steps. Then Ray turned all the way around directly toward us again and said to me,

"Get the next part for me babe…cuz I'm…crapped out."

And he fired a bullet through his heart, falling into the heart shaped pool sinking toward the ring.

THE END

2 - Trapped Five-O

A sparrow flew atop the showerhead by the pool. The odd thing was, the man noticed from his balcony, its position, perched between the pipe and the showerhead--between filth and cleanliness. Jonesie looked harder, leaning forward, and saw that the tiny bird took a minute, watery dump. It had settled for filth the man concluded. But you could not blame him for it was only a bodily function that must take priority. He had to laugh. Shit. Yes. That was the word--what he had been in and was in. Yet only a few more hours remained to shed out of this sheepdip his code word for parole; it was to be all over at midnight.

'So why sweat it?' Parole was almost over. Sean, his lawyer friend had asked him, as he was about to embark upon its terms. 'Two years. How hard could it be? You stayed out of trouble your whole life until you were twenty-eight.'

'That was luck,' he had replied to Sean.

I could go out. No harm in going to the pool hall. And what's more, I've always been safe there, Jonesie reasoned. There, the people always got my back.

Lieutenant Jademan stuffed the Playboy into the sofa, but where would he put the smutty video? It was too big. He could always put it in his locker at the station. No. Too risky for the spot inspections that the new police captain had been implementing lately. So he pulled the cop car by the coffee shop's alley and stuffed it against the wall, pinned behind the gutter.

Over the radio, a dispatch came. He had to meet a bunch of cops. There'd be a sting tonight. They were to meet in the parking plaza across from the pool hall. He wrapped up the cruller.

Jonesie hustled a few players then went back for a pitcher. He joked and made friends easily with the tourist til he lit a big stogie and pissed everybody off. He went back to the table and mercurially ran a bunch of balls. Jonesie was happy for he made lots of money; relaxing, about to go back for his second, but last pitcher, for he wanted to be clearheaded when midnight came around, whereupon something caught his eye.

The megaphone blared. "Sam! Sam Jademan. Get in formation." Lt. Jademan had parked in the wrong spot and in the wrong direction. He turned off the radio and was about to back it up when he heard a leak. He paced around the car, noticed the flat in the rear driver's side, and looked up at the lights in the pool hall window. Sam was too embarrassed to bring it to the captain's attention. The captain was always pissed at him, telling him he didn't know how to change a flat, which was of course true. But the captain, being at the right place at the right time--always in the bad guys' faces.

Jademan's equipment was ragged and he never carried a spare tire, further exacerbating his current condition. The reason he gave the captain for not carrying a spare was preposterous. Jademan claimed that 'a spare would make his car too heavy in speed-chases.' The captain, remembering this episode, shook his head now as he looked askance at the lieutenant, who had been staring at the pool hall's lights for some time, then alternately pacing around his car.

The lieutenant's thoughts were that the captain'd yell at him in front of the rest of the cops. He never minded being berated by the man, one-on-one, but he had a hard time being humiliated in front of a parking lot full of cops. Simply put, he was paranoid of group humiliation.

Jonesie looked at the cop looking at the pool hall--staring for a minute or two. It shot a pang of panic up and down him. He took a gigantic gulp from the pitcher to put his heartbeat right again. He turned away toward the television, which couldn't hold his attention. Antsily, he asked the bartender if people could see in through the windowpane. Jonesie had peered through numerous times at night and knew people were visible, illuminated in the green swag lights. But, what of discernment during the day? Or particularly twilight? He asked the bartender, Oscar, who didn't allay his fears when he answered, 'he thought so,' to Jonesie. Jonesie dipped his brown Irish scalli-cap over his blue eyes, which twinkled as he saw another mick, Johnny.

For a second opinion, Jonesie opined, "Johnny, let me ask you--can anyone see in here during the day…and late afternoon?"

"I don't think so." Johnny turned to go back to his game, looked over his shoulder and added, "You alright, Jonesie?"

Jonesie was embarrassed at the question. For he prided himself on being as cool, or nearly as collected as Johnny. But the pang began to unravel his insides as he looked at all the cop cars aligned. And that one damned cop still looking up at Jonesie. Shit. I think he made eye contact---the bartender was right. He needed to talk to Johnny even if it wasn't true; a fellow bloke to tell him it was all right. Damn these windows. Why hadn't he really paid attention to the site-line detail upon entering at this hour before? Twilight--always a difficult time to see clearly. He remembered reading or hearing about this from a news report about traffic accidents occurring mostly at dusk.

His concerns now were on the 5-0 traffic across the parking lot. He had a birds-eye view. But the damned cop's vision kept periscoping up from the hot, parking lot ground. The bird could be trapped; that was his fear, renewed stronger now though. He fled to the bartender.

"Hey Oscar. I think those cops over there are after me." Jonesie felt a wave of relief off his chest, putting his offense on another. But he knew this freeing feeling would be fleeting as Oscar spoke. "Why?"

"Well, last night…"

And Jonesie crossed his arms tightly; all bore up for the story.

"…I met this Black girl at that Irish bar, Casey's. And I think she was a crackhead because when we got out of there at dawn, after drinking Dewar's, a police car suddenly emerged beside a telephone pole from across the street. And another one in the direction of the trailer park just west converged there too. So, I peeled out discreetly and drove across the street to avoid them. We pulled off the side of the road and she kept asking me what we were doing there. I told her about my parole being nearly over and my need to stay out of trouble."

"I told you not to drink so much, especially at night bro," Oscar lectured, thinking this was another mick who never knew when to quit.

"I know. I had soda at first, but this girl seduced me. I hadn't had Dewars for so long. He took a sip of beer and was sure that the cop would be coming up the stairs any minute. "Listen Oscar, if a cop comes up here, can I hide in the back-room here?"

"Sure, no problem." Like it was no big deal--that softened his fears for a moment. But then he analyzed it in his mind further and turned it strange and ludicrous.

Oscar left to clean the bathroom. Jonesie pivoted often, trying to concentrate on watching the bar for Oscar, which calmed him until his next pivot. He yo-yo'd like this for awhile. Oscar came back and said, "Why don't you try to relax? Go home."

"I can't."

"Why?"

"Because they're out there, Jonesie explained.

Oscar bit his lip apparently understanding the man's paranoia then fed, "You feel if you go out there, they will stop you."

"Yes," Jonesie replied automatically and brushed his forefinger and thumb roughly pulling his scalli-cap forward with enough force that his head jutted forward from the pressure of the tug.

"Well, I would just go. You did nothing wrong. Right?"

Jonesie's scalli-cap tripped vertically from the knuckle side of his peace-fingers which flicked the visor and made a thudding-crack sound though only audible to close-by Oscar thereafter saying,

"They might think I was trying to cop some drugs with her. I could be an accomplice. She was acting crazy man."

He didn't tell Oscar the part about him remaining in a holding pattern parked outside the bar, moving only slightly back and forth along the same pavement spots, and delaying taking her home for fear of the cops' possible pursuit.

Jonesie flashed back to when he accused her of being a druggie when she went to use the bathroom as he was waiting fifteen feet off in the car, kitty-corner to the bar in the vicinity of the same crossed-over pavement before he had pulled out between the crossing police cars.

"I didn't buy drugs from them,"--she insisted. "Geez! And I thought I was bad. You got real issues honey."

In the car this accusation had really bothered him. He was superior to her and she had drug him beneath her with that statement. And it killed him. But now, it was a distant problem in comparison to the cops swarming around outside.

To compound matters considerably,

Johnny came over and said, "Yeah, I think the cops are looking over here. There's another one, just pulled closer."

Lt. Jademan had moved closer after persuading a pizza deliverer to fix his tire.

Jonesie watched the lieutenant move closer and exclaimed to himself, "Fuck. Now I'm screwed." Paranoia ratcheted up and down his spine and gripped him with a stranglehold on his heart and his protruding Adam's apple.

He jumped off the stool and began pacing. Johnny went back to his game, but Jonesie needed to talk to some one. He still wanted to remain cool, even though Oscar probably thought he was insane. But he thought of the cops coming upstairs. How would it be? How long before they came in the back room? Would they ask Oscar for his description? Would Oscar crack under pressure and give them his address? Where would he go? Was his attorney's number in his pocket? If so what good would that do him anyway? For he was out of state.

More questions snowed him under further. Here in this heat--this June Miami heat. He had forgotten to ask Oscar to turn on the A/C. But Jonesie had sweated so much.

What'd be the point for cool air now? 5-O might be hauling his ass in soon. He remembered years ago the feel of the cool cuffs as if it were yesterday. Some things you never forget. Jail a second time would be worse, especially down here. The variety of monsters from all over South Florida, from other states, hardened city criminals. And he had no connections locally to shorten his sentence in a plea situation. He was on his own in the back room. For the back room was his only hope-- the only way out. If the cops came in that room he'd be trapped. He'd have to break out the porthole window since it was on the main street. But the cops would be on him before his feet hit the pavement. That small room would be his only hope--his last stand. He'd always vowed that he'd never go to jail a second time- -that he'd kill whoever the cop was that'd try to detain him. So how would he react now that it was happening? Oh God. It was happening. He screamed to the insides of his bones-- shaking out of control now. He needed to stop shaking. Raul, the newspaperman whom he had always spoken with at the pool hall, approached Jonesie after the game in which the scoop man had been playing ended.

"Raul!" Jonesie rejoiced. "Do me a favor--

are you leaving now?" making the prospect seem more irresistible than an extended deadline for a Monday morning edition.

"No. Why?"

"I need some one to shield me from those cops."

"Why? What did you do?"

"I can tell you're a journalist with all the questions. Listen--I got mixed up with some woman and I think she was in some type of drug ring..."

"Oooh yeah. Stay away from that by all means. I heard a leak in the paper that they were doing a bust."

"Where?!" Jonesie's curiosity bordered on the maniacal.

"Plantation."

That did it.

Jonesie commanded, "O.K. Let's go downstairs. You're big enough to shield me. Just give me your windbreaker and cap for a disguise."

Raul surveyed him like the crazy man he knew he was devolving into. But composure took a long backseat to his panic mode. Damn. No pussy was worth this heightened state of anxiety now. He had reveled in observing the large black men ogle the black beauty queen he was with last night--a great roll in the hay by the wayside; for he only got brief tongue upon dropping her off in front of her trailer. He'd gotten popped for that kiss. Not in the chops, but she'd wailed on his shoulder with a lightning quick roundhouse that bruised his right shoulder. She'd have been a physical lay. Maybe too much for him. He regretted not speaking to her in the morning. For she had left a phone message when he awoke, but he was fearful to pick up the receiver thinking that she'd be calling him from jail and need his help to get bailed out. He was sure of it, though he did want to see her--not just for the sex either. She had opened up to him. So that tears flowed freely as she confessed, "Why am I telling you all this personal stuff? I don't even know you."

He recalled probing nicely at first, then harshly into areas of her previously off limits psyche. She broke down and they became closer in that brief amount of time than either ever had, even toward other prior lovers in their lives.

But he couldn't think of that tenderness now, or a sense of betrayal would dull his senses, which he needed acutely now for he had 5-O in his face instead. The bastards!

Forever threatening ruin. And now possibly to end his life, for all intents and purposes, permanently.

Raul tapped him on the shoulder. "Jonesie, let me buy you a beer. You're too tense. It's probably nothing. Oscar, put it on my tab."

"Yeah I guess you're right," Jonesie answered Raul and went to the bar to receive his beer. He sipped it and felt slightly better. Then he realized it was basically dark now. The swag lights would give hime away. He shrunk to the far side of the bar and was careful not to look behind him toward the wide-open window, for the girl may have given the police a description of him. Fuck. That cleared it in his mind. Jonesie thought of which prison and what the paddy wagon ride would be like on the way to jail.

The porkchop, sideburned Captain, holding the megaphone approached Lt. Jademan.

"What are you looking at? We've been holding this sting operation for the last five minutes without you. I know you feel like you can sniff out the drugs like some damned bloodhound, but you do need to be briefed on the logistics at the least. Let's go."

The lieutenant felt the Captain's hand turn him at this point, but he continued staring as a statue, gazing at the pool hall windows up afar.

"What?" shouted the Captain.

"Something's going on up there. Some one's trapped."

"Trapped--who?"

"Like a little lamb or pig squealing," Jademan commented more to himself than the Captain. "You want me to check it out?" as Jademan stepped toward the pool hall hypnotically.

"You're not going anywhere, cept with me. Come on. The blue crew is waiting for you...and your upturned nostrils."

Johnny came over to Jonesie. "I don't think they're waiting for you. They're walking to the other building."

Jonesie looked to Raul who was busy lining up a shot and suddenly Jonesie decided to risk it. He made it to the door but became paralyzed. He spotted a goateed bald man round the corner with a hefty woman. This is it! This is it! The cops!! They skirted the right side of the mall and now are making their way up the spiral staircase. They were cops. Yes definitely. The goateed man had held an oversized baton. Oh no. I've been beaten with those badly before. And this guy looks like a bad-ass, probably was in the Marines, or a Seal, or both. Jonesie alarmed everyone by running into the bathroom. Raul raised his eyebrows to Oscar who shrugged. Jonesie listened as the door closed. He kept waiting. Silence. No greetings.

Maybe the cops were looking for Oscar, who maybe had gone into the backroom to heat up his dinner. Or maybe the cops were whispering to him about Jonesie. Shit. It'd be a matter of seconds. He braced himself. Ears pressed against the bathrooms turquoise-chipped thick paint. Then he realized there was no escape route in this shithouse. He examined the ceiling. No--an escape held no promise whatsoever. He'd have to assault the cop. But there wasn't just one. The female. She looked through the glass too.

He waited, waited some more. Then suddenly a blast shook from right outside the door, which remained open. It was of the type that wouldn't lock. Just Jonesie's luck. He was Irish without the 'luck of' applicable as a precedent for his charm. This explosion riveted Jonesie's pulse, wiring it and wrenching his heart at once, as it beat faster than an Ingve Malmstein guitar solo; everything amplified and on overload. He sweated it til he realized a millisecond later that it was the damn jukebox, "BAP-BAP, BAP-BAP," thundered as a prelude to Jonesie's favorite play, Aerosmith's 'Eat the Rich.' This with the music seemed normal now. But there were cops in here; Jonesie more than suspected, he could feel it, their presence, authoritative and tired. He'd have to make his escape to the beat of the jukebox. He found this an odd, yet strangely comforting thought, than perhaps it would have necessitated in silence. Why hadn't anyone approached him yet? How long had it been? Dare he peek? No. He couldn't. He was certain he'd see a revolver pointing at him, or the big baton wielded nonchalantly by the cue-balled cop, itching to give Jonesie a beating. No. Don't look. If you look you'll know; then you're doomed Jonesie--doomed. Life as you know it is over. Fuck! And to think at midnight he'd have been off parole-- just a few hours away. 'What bad timing,' his mind scolded him unrelenting. Every time I try to celebrate. Damn. Something bad happens. So I can't. So I can't. Ooh! He fumed. Just look. Be brave. Be brave. Yeah, but you can never be brave again-- in here again. You acted like a coward in front of Raul, Johnny, Oscar, everyone in here. Compose yourself. Just look. He inched closer. He looked. He was relieved. It was only Christy and Bruno. How could he have mistaken them for cops? The huge baton was merely Bruno's cue covered in its black holster. Phew!

"Have a drink Jonsie. Man, you look pale," Bruno commented.

"Yeah, I've had the shits all day--nasty."

"Pour one from the pitcher for my man Jonsie," Bruno directed Christy who poured.

"How ya doin' Jonessie?" she asked.

"Okay. Hey, tell me. What's going on down there?" as Jonesie pointed to the littered lot.

"Don't know. Why?" she returned.

Oscar interjected, "Jonesie thinks the cops are after him."

"Why?" asked Christy.

He told them the story. Bruno listened with interest and mentioned that he had friends on the department.

"Great. Then you can escort me down there in case there's any problem."

It was all settled in Jonesie's mind. An

angel sent just for him. A bona fide miracle.

Jonesie turned, put his arm around Bruno and walked toward the door. After a step and a half, he realized he was alone. Bruno hadn't followed his lead.

"Aren't you going to drink your beer?" Christy asked to Jonesie's astonished blues, which were accentuated above with his thin eyebrows arching for the swag's light above.

"Now? I've gotta leave. I might even call that girl back." Then to Bruno, "Let's go Bruno. If you don't mind--before you get into your game. But Bruno's back had been turned for a time and he had broke already.

Jonesie knew Bruno never abandoned a game he started. But in this exigent circumstance he pleaded.

"Bruno--weren't you listening? I've got to get out of here. Those cops are planning on coming up here--For Me!"

"Jonesie," Bruno smiled. "Those cops would've been up here already if they wanted to arrest you. Just go ahead out."

Jonesie hadn't thought of this. It comforted him. Immensely comforted him A wave of relief came over him. The lines in his face loosened. Christy smiled at his relief.

"Yeah but...No no. They might be

bringing her up to identify me. They're waiting for the girl. Women are always late, excuse me Christy. Yeah, that's why."

It dawned on him. That's why she called me this morning--to set me up.

"It's a sting. I knew it. They're always doing drug stings around here. Beforehand, Raul even told me about one that was expected. This is the one. This is the one." He felt himself convincing the others; with each sentence the doubt about Jonesie's paranoia receded amongst them, registering less and less upon his audience's faces. Yes. Jonesie was right about being the scapegoat. Alas...He had convinced them.

"Well, there are a lot of stings," Bruno conceded.

Aha, Jonesie's inner consciousness leapt for joy. Bruno continued, "But I really don't think so."

"You don't thinks so!: Jonesie's anger ignited and overtook the best of him. "What if I go down there and they pick me up? How's that going to make you feel?" He looked at Johnny.

Bruno counseled, "Don't worry. I think they really would have been here for you already if that was the case. Cops don't play."

"Yeah, you think. You think. That's the

whole issue. You think they don't play, but you don't know. That's their whole game, to play and fuck with people's lives. You think, yet *you* don't get it." He paused enough to soften, "Help me out--at least walk me to the door. My car is right underneath here. Quick."

"Uh-oh," Christy declared ominously.

"What?" Jonesie sidestepped into her face quickly.

"The cops pointing at the window," she mentioned with a note of alarm. "Hey, isn't that a megaphone?"

Jonesie spilt his beer.

"Shit," and ran to the backroom, past Oscar. He hurriedly wrote down his parents' hone number and gave it to Oscar. "Let them know if I go back to jail."

"O.K. O.K."

This reaction panicked Jonesie even more--like jail for him was a foregone conclusion on this eve. Jonesie looked out the wide porthole window. It's not too far to jump. I may have to. What am I going to use to break the window? Oscar will be pissed but I've gotta do it.

Still in the backroom, he waited for the megaphone to be used. What would the voice sound like? Would it be a sudden storming of chaotic rumblings? Or would they send the girl in, as bait?

"Is there a black girl approaching here?" he yelled to Oscar. He must've made his rounds, grabbing the glasses left by patrons on the surrounding tables. Finally, a voice. A female voice. Jonesie held his breath:

"There's none here."

He exhaled. Ahh, it was only Christy.

Jonesie retold the story to her though unasked, just to calm himself down. She looked upon him sympathetically.

"Why won't Bruno walk me down? You've got to convince him."

After a moment, she excused herself without a word. Under his dipped scalli, Jonesie's eyes followed her.

"Damn!" The bathroom." Jonesie could scarcely believe it. What the fuck! How can she go to the bathroom to shit--when I've been shitting my brains for hours now?

He inched out of the room, sat at the bar, which he tapped for awhile; then looked in the mirror, turned around, and studied the parking lot. It could be safe. He could do it. He might even make it to his car. They weren't too close; but he couldn't see directly underneath to where his car beckoned. Then a more frightening thought. The cops could be in the coffee shop directly underneath the pool hall. Those pigs are probably packed in that place more than they've filled that lot. His heart sank. But he couldn't *think* anymore. Jonesie raced out the door whereupon a rush as if from a showerhead hit his cap threatening to knock off his scalli-cap.

THE END

3 - Cold French Fries

"You'd wrap two pieces of bread around...Spaghetti," Anthony joked seriously to Bones.

"What can I say--I love sandwiches."

"Well you eat too many. And it shows."

They came in off the porch, which overlooked the pool on the warm Massachusetts night.

"Are you and Bud still going to Montreal next weekend?" Anthony asked.

"Buuurp." Bones wiped the mayonnaise off his mouth and smoothed out his ample belly, while Anthony opened the door underneath the kitchen sink and threw some fast food wrappers in the basket, helping Bones clean up all the late night junk food he'd consumed.

Anthony laughed while Bones started his answer.

"I don't know. I'll call him. He knew the other three cancelled, but he thought you were going. So…I'll call him this week and see.

"All right. If you go have a good time…And be careful!"

Their group met at 'The Venice' the next night, Thursday, without Anthony, who had a hoop game with his work colleagues.

"I'm nervous Bones said to Wrinkled Rob. They stood by the Golden Tee golf video game in the dimly lit corner of the bar section of the restaurant/sports bar called The Venice.

Bones was comfortable in this venue. He'd been a 'Venice' patron along with his family since he was seven. Gradually, and inevitably some may say, The Venice morphed into his second home, particularly the bar portion. He'd tell his parents he was visiting Wrinkled Rob but three quarters of the time, Bones would end up meeting him at said bar know for pizzas and softball celebrations.

The two watched Bulge and Rich play.

"What are you nervous about?" Bones asked Wrinkled Rob, who never ironed a shirt. Anthony had coined the nickname--behind his back.

"Well," he said from under his blue corduroy cap, "I think the two of you going up there alone spells trouble."

"I know. I know," he said in his calm and most convincing tone to match Wrinkled's drone manner; their Ivy League analysis always in sync. You think he's too much of a loose cannon?"

"We've seen evidence a number of times," Wrinkled Rob pressed. And you two won't have Bulge here available to bail you out up there if Bud goes off."

Bulge finished beating Rich and sauntered over. "What? And you're a calmer drunk?"

Bulge surprised Bones with his tone; the friendly brogue was raised slightly accusatory, apparently ready for a verbal skirmish pitting the Harvard Law grad against the Columbia engineering grad.

"I've got more control than Bud. Did you hear what he did last week?" Bones asked.

"It was a long week," Bulge answered tongue in cheek.

"He's talking about when Bud got in a fight with cops," Wrinkled answered.

"Plain clothed--they didn't identify themselves when he was fighting that first guy," Bones now defended Bud.

"He spat blood like an animal on the cop's desk," continued Wrinkled. "Rich here was in the adjacent room and had to break into it when the cop that Bud punched came in."

"Yeah, I talked him down with Anthony who they tried to book too," explained Rich.

"Ahh--but you got out of the clink. Tony made mention of it on the phone; a minor disorderly that didn't stick."

"Ya, but Bud was an instigator. He no sooner than bumped into the guy than he wound up instantaneously on the other fighter."

"I heard," Bulge laughed, "that it looked like Rocky versus Clubber Lang in that slo-mo shot where they go for the simultaneous knockout punch. Don't sweat it. You'll be fine." He directed the latter comment to Bones. "Bud's easy to manage one-on-one. Just stick together. Hell, you've known him all your life. And you know how to talk to him better than anyone."

"Don't tell me--tell Rob here. He's the one

harping on the issue."

"I just think he acted like an animal, especially when he was detained. You better hope no boys'n blue are up there cuz he can't stay calm with them. Bud acts like an animal, especially on tequila."

"You boys are going to Montreal not Mexico," reminded Bulge and slapped Bones on his thick back. "An animal?" You might as well be talking about this guy here," Bulge continued to Rob directing comments to Bones.

"Why?" Wrinkled smoothed his plaid, dappled grunge shirt before looking up to address Bulge, sporting a large grin.

"I'll tell you a story--Ha ha," his large frame bent over; Kennedy-esque features radiated warmth amongst the bar and all ears seemed to adhere to Bulge's berthing charisma. "Bones, my brother, and myself went up to Montreal for New Year's last year. Bones gets liquored up at a strip bar all afternoon. And some girl he's been tipping hard the whole time...Ha ha!" Bulge doubled over again. "... I mean dropping wads of bills, large bills; and after each deposit the girl whispers what she plans to do to him afterward--because I gather she told Bones here that her shift ended at six p.m.--so Bones waits. My brother's getting hungry and decides to get some dinner. Bones keeps drinking his Molson XX bottles and next thing he knows it's nine o'clock. He figures the girl has gone home. But he goes in to take a leak--comes out, heads for the exit, and out of the corner of his eye, Bones sees the girl giving a guy a lap dance--a real raunchy one. So Bones sits there watching, waiting for it to end. Ha ha ha--and it doesn't end; the guy keeps her there song after song. Bones is freaking. He eats a sandwich, watching her and the guido guy the whole time, getting madder with each song that passes. She then gets up to perform on the main stage, when they call her name--ha ha. What was it?"

Bulge glanced to Bones, whose head remained down throughout the account, but his hush-puppy-dog eyes rolled upward and said, "SuperMeg."

Wrinkled Rob's pale thin face expressed a smile with a short, snorty laugh.

"So Bones is blocking her way to the stage and mumbles, "Shift over?"

"She looks at him kind of funny because he's so drunk that he can barley speak. She goes, "Oh, I'm sorry I told the manager I'd work a double."

"Then Bones says, 'So, I'll stay here until it's over, then take you home.' Sure stay--she tells Bones. And he does."

At this point in Bulge's story, Bones' head sinks even lower in pain, until it lay parallel to the Venice table, an inch away from the red and white tablecloth.

"Bones wait's the entire time until the place closes. And he'd fallen asleep and opens his eye to see the guy who'd been stealing all his table dances, going home with SuperMeg."

Now Bones spoke.

"Ah, but she was so hot--a little blond that Hummm," he flared out his right forearm, elbow first, cracking it hard against his left palm, making a sound like a cap gun. Bones clenched his teeth down and continued in a sexual frustration tizzy, "Little sexy blond, tattoo of a Bruin's logo on her ass," repeating, "Hummmm," further frightening the small bar crowd; though the regulars had witnessed the sophomoric theatrics in accustomed nightly doses. "I'll tattoo ya--Hummm."

Wrinkled Rob and Bulge both doubled over in gorged laughter.

Rob said, "Yeah, but that's not as

animalistic as Bud."

"No, but you haven't heard the funny part. My brother gets back to the hotel and we wait up for Bones. Finally, we turn off the lights and go to sleep. We're awakened to see Bones with ketchup smeared on his lips, muttering, 'dumb bitch.'"

"What went wrong Bones?" my brother asked. "I thought you were going to score that chick with the Bruins logo."

"As an aside, my brother began to tell me about the time he and Bones were watching the Eastern Conference finals with the Edmonton Oilers against the Bruins. Bones was screaming at the television all night and when the clock expired with the Bruin's losing, he gunned a pen at the T.V. His dad, who never says a thing, goes, 'easy killer.' Bones goes, 'you don't understand…'

Bulge switched gears now continuing, "Then Bones whips his McDonalds's wrapper into the basket and proceeds to go on a tirade, telling us the whole story with the chick. And more. With each detail he becomes madder and madder. By the time he reaches the point where SuperMeg leaves with guido, Bones here, in a fit of super-human strength, kicks one of those large, what we had previously thought was grounded, thick T.V. chair with that heavy wood base and all, clear across the room!..."

"My brother and I just stood there with our mouths open. Then Bones proceeds to walk over to the bucket and unwrap the McDonald's liner and finish the rest of his chicken sandwich, or whatever the hell it was."

Rob laughed tears. And Bones said, "They were French fries."

"That reminds me of the time that Bones came to a party with me and Beaker at Boston University," Wrinkled grinned.

"What happened?" asked Bulge.

"He was walking around outside, lost..."

"I knew where I was," rose Bones staunchly.

"Well, you were looking all around you outside Beaker's apartment." Wrinkled continued to Bulge, "A mountie pulls up on a horse and he radios back to the station. And I can hear him cuz by this time Bones is like two doors down from Beaker's place. Before I can yell to him, I hear the cop speaking into his walkie-talkie, 'Yeah, Serge--we've got a stocky, balding Caucasian, he actually resembles George Castanza on that Seinfeld show; he has mayonnaise on his mouth, a burger roll hanging out of his mouth, and has been kicking a Burger King bag from one side of the street to another for three city blocks, has been causing a disturbance, barking angry comments to no one--just kicking his bag in tote--and acting like a…a general primate."

Rich chuckled heartily and volunteered, "Those last two words are an accurate description. I remember the time he'd just finished a late night snack from Arby's and he couldn't wait to use the bathroom…"

Bones' head went down at this point all the way on the red checkered table--specifically on the placemat menu with a black gondola printed on it.

Rich turned back to Bulge, "And I said, 'it's just two minutes Bones,' cuz we'd just pulled off the highway. Every ten seconds, he's saying 'pull over, I can't make it.' Eventually, I say, 'it's a minute and a half away.' Ha ha. I look over and he's turning blue in the passenger seat. I say, 'Under a minute--here's your side street; just hold on big fella.' He grabs the wheel, grimacing and grunting no-- and I say, 'Okay, I'm stopping now.' I pull over just beyond the Burnett's yard and figure he's going to walk deep behind the Burnett's side yard for more shelter, you know."

"Yeah?" said Bulge, continuing to stare in amazement for he seemed to be predisposed to listen with particular care to people with dump stories of any sort. He smiled and leaned further in.

"But what does Bones do? I'm in the middle of changing the radio dial, look in the yard, and see him right in front, clear as day, in the Burnett's side yard, squatting with each hand held tightly on two trees flanking him, and his trousers around his ankles. And just this menacing grimace--like, 'Yeah!' which matched his shout, roared Rich emulating Bones' relief.

Bulge laughed, slapped Bones on the back, "Like a bear shitting in the woods, huh Bonesie," Bulge commented. We've gotta get you a pooper scooper."

"Relax chief," uttered Bones. "I thought we were discussing Bud's social problems."

Rich chimed in to switch to one of Bud's anecdotes. "Bud. Ha. Remember Bones, when we went to visit you at Columbia when the Patriots played the Bears--Da Bears." Rich couldn't resist mimicking Chris Farley, with his grizzly-adams, goateed, kind face.

Bones nodded.

"We were unpacking late at night," Rich unfolded. "You must've been brushing your teeth Bones. In the car, Bud had been trying to sleep before we got into New York. So he conks out immediately. And Anthony grabs his shaving kit cuz he wants to see if he's got any toothpaste so he can go brush his teeth. And Bud evidently woke up and we hear this voice in the dark...that at the time we didn't recognize as Bud's. And he breaks the whole dorm wing's silence with, "Put that down!"

"Anthony says, 'Cool it. I'm only looking for toothpaste.' There's a slight pause--and Bud bellows even louder in a thunderous voice, 'PUT THAT DOWN!" like there's some rare jewel in his ratty old shaving kit. Anthony thought it was hilarious."

"See. That's a harmless story," Bulge summarized; this story not revving his engine like DaBear's shit story had. "At least he didn't kick any furniture. "So is it settled Bones? You going to call Bud to venture north?"

Bones stepped to the payphone and dialed Bud's number.

"You two maniacs have a good time," Bulge said as he watched Bones drop in the coins.

"He hasn't said yes yet," Bones replied steadily.

"Bud will though," Rich issued as Bulge nodded.

On the plane, Bones put his beer on the coaster and perused Bud's profile. Bud was reading; the magazine brushing against the tray in front of him which also held an empty peanut wrapper. Looking like a tanned Frenchman, Bud's glow overshadowed Bones' paleness.

"Any peanuts left Bud?"

"No. They give you like three and you want one from me. I already ate them--jackass."

Bones smiled and paused for the right way to address a potentially sensitive issue.

He began with a sigh, "Listen, it's just the two of us up here. So let's make a pact." He turned to Bud, who studied Bones' golf hat and then settled his unsettling eyes on Bones' brown, steady, hush-puppie colored, open, knowing pupils.

"What?"

"That we'll keep both our behaviors in check. Let's just have a nice relaxing time up in Montreal."

"Yeah. Well, we got tickets to the Astros Expos game--how much trouble can we get into at a ball game. Do your Rich Gedman imitation. It's even funnier now that that catcher got traded from our hometown BoSox to Houston."

Bones laughed, "Maybe later Bud." After sipping his drink then added, "Just remember stud, the Astros game is only three hours. We still have quite a bit of down time to get in trouble."

"I promise I'll be good," Bud reassured. "Besides, we'll be together. We'll watch each other like hawks--you astronaut."

Bud slipped the magazine back into the seat's flap and reached under his window seat for a manila envelope to read something he'd written in college. He needed to laugh. Though he was very comfortable with Bones, he wasn't sure if they'd weather Montreal well at all.

Bud tried not to think of the time in Florida at 'The Candy Store,' where he had to run out of line, after insulting a bouncer and a cop at the door to get in. He ran for blocks and lost them miraculously by diving underneath a truck on a side street. He'd been close to mowing lawns for a summer down there. Anyway, that's what he'd heard how law enforcement treats rebellious northerners down there. On the plane, he now read the first paragraph of 'Fred, Johnny and Derek's Delirious Dialogue'; Bruins announcers he and his cousin Munch had scoffed at the sometimes absurd, but always hilarious utterances, and came up with a long, printed list of funny comments made by the partisan Beantown television announcers--Fred Cuestick, Johnny Penpoint, and Derek Sanderson. He read the first blurb:

Derek: (after Burin Sweeney lost a close fight to a Vancouver Canuck) "You have to give Sweeney the decision."

Fred: "Why?"

Derek: "Because--he's tougher. Anytime you're regarded as a tough guy, as VanDork is, and you don't win the fight outright--you know decisively, then in my book--you lose.

Fred: "The Bruins haven't lost a

fight all year--right Derek?"
Derek: "Yes they have."

Bud read the next one avidly:

Derek: "Great save by Roy."
Fred: "I believe that's pronounced 'Ra-Wah,' Derek."
Derek: "Well, he's in the states now--and from where we come from that's ROY!"

And lastly:

Johnny Penpoint: "I would venture to say the three best teams in the National Hockey League are, number one--the New York Islanders, number two--the Montreal Canadians, and number three, the ALL AMERICAN...Edmonton Oilers. (Edmonton au Canada of course).

These took Bud's mind away from possibilities of trouble and wished simply that there were a Habs-Bruins game; a classic match of brawny body checks and fiery fore-checking. Astros-Expos seemed just too...pacifying.

They checked into the hotel.

"Let me see your keys--mine's stuck," Bones required.

"Give me a minute." Bud put his half-full Bud-bottle on the veranda next to Bones' near empty Molson XX.

"Hurry."

"Why? What's you're rush?"

"I've got to take a leak."

"Oh. Presto, open sesame--see!" Bud grinned and thought of how much fun this trip would be as they walked into their room It already was a success; his buzz on since the plane ride ensued and no sign of leaving. Plus, their dollar could go far in bars down here.

They approached Olympic Stadium. Concrete bars everywhere.

"Hmm, a lot less glamorous and not nearly as green as Fenway. No Fenway Franks either," Bud complained as he loved the broiled dogs since his early youth.

"Who gives a fuck grumpy? They've got cold beer. That's all I give a shit about."

"Right," Bud nodded, content to gaze down by his feet; two beers mine, two beers his--perfect.

"I've got to find the restroom," Bones scrambled up squeezing by Bud.

After numerous alternating rounds down the aisle for pour-ins and inevitably pour-outs, Bud remembered something during the seventh inning stretch.

"Oooh--I almost forgot. Do Rich Gedman."

Bones rose to join Bud on his feet; Bud glanced down with glee to the face which was about to morph into Rich Gedman.

"Haha. Perfect. Like you've just bitten into a lemon. I wish I could see Gedman to see just how much you resemble him. I shoulda brought binoculars--damn!"

"That's all there is to it, sucking on a lemon," his face back to normal now.

"Speaking of lemons--tequila tonight," Bud warned.

"No fucking way man. Remember our pact."

Bud wanted to say lighten up, but sat back down to watch the last of the inning.

However, they didn't stay for the last two innings. For they wanted to get a head start on the serious strip joint activity before hitting the late night 'normal clubs' to maximize the fun on their short pleasure trip.

"What are these?" asked Bud during dinner.

"Frites de…or French fries."

Bud was going to repeat en francaise, but wasn't sure of the pronunciation, though he'd taken French and Bones had just said it, albeit with his mouth full of potato and gravy.

"Hmm. Nice and warm," Bud tasted them.

"Goes good with Molson XX, eh?"

"Eh," Bud echoed in his best McKenzie Brothers impression. "Speaking of X's, which strip club should we hit?"

"I browsed through a magazine earlier in the lobby. There's a chick who puts out a lighter stuck in a bottle by squatting and queefing over it. I think I remember the address."

"That's it?"

"Well, the whole show is quick. But the chick is amazingly gorgeous. Trust me, she'll hold your attention."

They went. And she did. Though the lighting and the packed crowd made it difficult to glean her act clearly.

"Let's go. I don't want to spend all my money here. We should save it for buying chicks' shots later at the discotheque," Bud reasoned.

The next club was much more fun for Bud. He finally broke the ice with a short energetic blond French girl. They shot vodka together as Offspring's, 'Keep Them Separated,' blared in the rustic club. He was about to reach out and grab her to plant one on her at the bar. But as he paid the bartender and reached to give her shot glass to her, she turned suddenly and said, "Oops, sorry-- better looking guy," as if she were obligated to leave the fun he thought they were enjoying.

"Fuck, let's get out of here," Bud found and broke to Bones as soon as the former inhaled both vodkas.

"Dig that blond chick dancing on the table!" Bones pointed and his eyes wide open resembled white, vertical, teetering full-eggshells.

Bud pulled away from the sight of his lost

French dame, who happened to be the one ogled by Bones presently.

"I don't want to," protest Bud. "There's a good discotheque right across the street. Let's hurry before the line's too long."

After being inside the disco awhile, Bud noticed Bones doing well with a well-dressed hot black lady. Bud got on the move downstairs. He flirted but the women rejected him en frustrating francaise. Half hours flew by--up and down stairs; he'd just passed Bones on the stairs. Didn't he? Bud didn't know where he was, absently leaning on the rail dead center on the stairs. He spotted a fashionable girl and danced with her. It went well. But then he saw her dance with another guy. He should've counted his blessings of dancing with the sandy haired banged girl with the Lynx-colored hat resembling a stylish trapper's cap.

Bones came by to buy a brew.

"But I want tequila," said Bud.

Bones' hackles became visible to him. But Bud gave him a sharp eye. Bones relented, saying,

"Okay, but please...just one of these. We

all know what happens when you drink more than one of these bad boys--Tasmanian devil."

"Don't worry."

This gave Bud the power he so desperately needed. He decided to muscle in on the French dweeb who'd stolen his Lynxy feline. Yeah it was true. The girl was smiling at him in his sway. She wanted him--not the whiny little French squid she was commiserating with. He followed the couple who were also accompanied by a few stragglers. Bud didn't know who they were; he thought he remembered her name so blurted," Tracy," as he reached for her.

Though recoiling in surprise, shocked at his brashness as Bud pulled her in closer to him by her wrist, away from her accoutrements and the taxi, she did not struggle.

"Where are you going?"

"St. Bonaventure Hotel," she replied.

"Good. I've never stayed there. They have a pool?"

Next thing he knew a cold ring clipped a chunk of skin underneath his chin.

Whoo. That was close. Bud didn't realize he was bleeding, but found himself in an argument with a black taxicab driver. How odd. How did people get in the cab so quick?

"Stay here," an employee of the discotheque advised him.

Bud moved to the car. "I'll kill you. You French fag...squid." The cab peeled off to the Bonaventure. He pondered the rides that he couldn't take and wouldn't make.

"Where are you going?" a voice rang as he stepped off the curb, his back to the disco.

"What?" Bud turned slowly around.

The bouncer asked again. "You have a friend?"

"Uh--no. I...I think he went home."

"Everyone did sir. It's three in the morning. You need to go to the hospital."

"Why? He only grazed me."

"You're bleeding."

"It's just a nick."

"No. Look at your collar. It's deep. I really think you ought to get it looked at." The man bent down while examining the chin closely underneath Bud.

Bud considered the number of fights the bouncer had witnessed and said, "Where's the nearest hospital?"

"Up that hill. It's not too far. You can walk it."

Bud walked to Montreal General Hospital

and wondered if the lengthy walk would be worth the surgical benefits. He flirted for three solid hours with the blond security guard to whom he'd relayed twice now his plight of the admissions person informing him that the wait could be from one to four hours--bitching about how a big city hospital could only have two doctors on.

"Isn't this a major city? I mean I know we're in Canada, but...and this is a Saturday night. What do they do when brawls break out?"

"Everyone minds their own business up here," the pony tailed blond explained. "Something like this is quite rare."

"Yeah, well I should be in the Bonaventure right now, but I gotta get stitched up instead. He felt like spitting, but realized she might take offense.

With his head down, she patted him on the leg, "I need to make my rounds."

"Sure. I will make a phone call."

Bud dialed the room. The phone rang forever. The man at the front desk came back on and told him their rooms were switched next door. He didn't think to ask why-- figured it was an overbooking oversight. He peeked to see if the girl returned from her rounds. The phone rang even longer when the clerk dialed the second room. Bud was about to hang up when he heard Bones' voice.

"Bones. It's Bud. I'm in Montreal General Hospital."

"That's nice. What're you doing there?"

"I got in a fight--need to get stitches. Where have you been?"

"Ha. I just got in." He seemed preoccupied. "You caught me when I just came in."

"From where?"

"Listen--I can't talk now. My French fries are getting cold."

Bud exasperated, wanted to tell him about the fight and how cowardly the French squid had hid..."

"So what I just...I'd like to talk to you Bud. But I can't stay on long."

"What do you mean you can't stay on long? You're not doing anything."

"I'm eating, or about to eat, ha. I got Micky D's."

Frustrated, Bud relented to the silliness, laughing to himself.

Bones explained, "I need to finish cuz I've got to call the front desk."

"For what--room service. You need more food?" Bud asked half-kidding.

"No. I broke down the door."

"You what?"

"I had to break down the door."

"What? Why? What do you mean you had to?"

"I already told you. My French fries were getting cold."

Bud didn't know whether to laugh or admonish him harshly, with his open chin smarting.

"How did you break it down?"

Now Bones' energy came to the forefront, jumping with excitement as Bud watched it become light outside the hospital waiting room.

"You'd have been proud Bud. I didn't have much room--cuz you know how small that veranda outside our room is…"

Bud couldn't believe he was pausing at this point in the story. "Ya," he gave Bones the verbal approval he evidently needed to proceed.

"Well, I pivoted, lowered my shoulder and BAM!"

"Bam what?"

"The door fell into the room as planned."

Bud laughed despite his irksomeness. "As planned? But what about your key? How did you lose it?"

"I didn't lose it. I've got it on me now still."

"Well, why didn't you use it Einstein?"

"Aww, come on. You remember how much trouble I had with it when we checked in."

"Ahh, no. Not really."

"We used your key to open it, remember?"

"But you didn't struggle with it. You've got to juggle keys. Don't you know that?"

"I guess I didn't have the patience for it."

"You didn't have the patience. How are we going to pay for this? I'm not mowing lawns up here in Canuck country until Labor Day."

"Ahh. Don't worry," control reentered Bones' voice. "Again, you'd be proud of me on this count especially."

Bud held his breath and the receiver tightly.

"I told the hotel manager that our room had been broken into. And…"

A female voice nearby Bud interrupted their phone conversation.

"Bud, the doctor can see you--admissions told me to tell you."

He winked at the security guard who had covered her ponytail with a blue cap now.

"Thank you honey," Bud took in a gander of the tautness of her slacks by her calves.

To Bones Bud returned saying, "Yeah, yeah. Smart thinking. Listen. Tell me the rest later." He could hear Bones continue to munch and talk into the receiver as he hung up the payphone.

"Cold French fries," he shook his head as the doctor stitched him up.

THE END

4 - Nomad Monks

We had a go on the Merry-Go-Round. It was during the spinning when it was decided I believe, or at least from it.

Stephen L. said to my brother, "I'm never going to get married."

Before my brother could reply I blurted out, "Me too."

"What do unmarried people do?" Stephen L. in his early youth beckoned.

We got off the merry-go-round and we all sadly watched its final rotation til it stopped. For we had had much fun and many laughs on this merry-go-round as did the older kids and adults. And we were always melancholy to step off it, being that we'd ridden it all summer long.

"I don't want to go to school," I said as those prior thoughts gave rise to the weighty statement.

"Chris, what would we do if we were unmarried?" Stephen L. asked my brother.

While Chris thought, I instinctively filled the silence, "We could go on a wild Safari to Africa," I said enthusiastically.

"We could never afford that," my brother pointed out.

"My uncle told me of missions that go over there--the Peace Corps I think. You can go there without paying he told my mom. That's how we could get there. I think we'd have to help sick people some time."

"That's a good idea Stephen L.," my brother commended the blond boy.

I thought this over and shook my head, "No. No. If we do that we might get sick too. What good would that be? Then we couldn't enjoy seeing all the animals if we caught whatever from those people."

"What else?" asked Stephen L.

I looked at my brother who picked at a green leaf. Since Chris's head remained down, I decided to suggest another alternative.

"We could all just live at one home together. This way we wouldn't have to come to pick up Stephen L. at his house in case he lived too far away. I pointed to my brother who looked up to his older brother instantly, "And you--you might live far away from me.

"So?" Chris answered.

"Don't you see? Unless we all live together," I stressed that word seemingly with my sprouting biceps, setting my authority on the two, "we wouldn't have to waste time picking each other up. We could all leave on an adventure each time together."

I watched for a reaction--Stephen L. seemed less threatened than the prior time my budding muscles retracted, but Chris was unmoved if he had even looked at me this time, "and have more time to spend there," I continued. "Right Stephen L.?"

Stephen L. confirmed my thought processes. "I would like to visit all the ball parks in the major league one summer."

"Yes." This I didn't even need to consider. "That should be our first adventure." I looked at Stephen L.'s St. Louis Cardinal hat and felt my Oriole cap and thought aloud, "Chris, you don't have a cap. If we're going to go on a trip to the baseball parks, you really oughta have a cap. A Bluejays cap will do just fine, eh?"

"Then what'll we do after that summer?"

my brother asked Stephen L.

Stephen L. looked blank a bit too long for my liking. I looked at the roundup ride and thought of rodeos.

I spoke, "The Wild West. We could take a trip to the Wild West--live one summer on a farm somewhere, and milk cows and lasso bulls. It'll be great fun!"

"It sounds like a good time. Sure. But we don't know anyone out west."

This stumped me. Stephen L. was right. I searched my memory. Optimistically, I asked,

"Chris, do we have any relatives out west?"

I saw him pulling the stem.

"Think. Think hard." I couldn't tell how hard he was thinking or if at all; he seemed more bored than usual.

Stephen L. then said, "We don't need to. We can hitchhike there and then find some one's farm. But then comes the hard part."

"What? What hard part?" I said somewhere in between annoyed and anxious.

"We've got to convince them to let us stay with them," said Stephen L.

"Shoot. That'll be a cinch. We just got to look the part. We'll buy some cowboy hats. And boots--we need those for our spurs.

That'll show'em we're real cowboys."

"How long would we stay?" Chris asked.

"Long enough. Til we've had all our adventures in the Midwest," I stated convincingly.

"How long is that?" Stephen L. challenged.

"Shoot, I don't know. It all depends on how much fun things there are there in the Midwest."

"Reason why is they may ask us to work to pay board," Stephen L. said.

"Yeah so? I told you I don't mind working a little." My bicep twitched with a nod of my will. "No problem, we'll get up early and mow the lawn some days and such." I noticed Stephen L. didn't look convinced.

"What's wrong Stephen L." That's a sound plan. Right Chris?"

Stephen L. issued, "I think I'd be scared if they had a shotgun."

"Why all farmers own one--to kill predators and looters," I explained.

"True enough, but I bet he could hold us hostage on that farm and make us slave laborers of some kind. Then we'd be stuck there forever. And I haven't any family to help bail me out of any trouble. It's too far."

"Arrgh!" I shrugged it off. As ringleader, I felt I had to show off my smarts too, to relieve Stephen L.

"Stephen L., a farm is so big that if we were doing chores on the far side of a wide acreage we'd have no trouble sneaking off the owner's ranch. Right Chris?"

My brother threw a rock that dinged the last picket of a white fence at the amusement park's edge, which we'd reached by the popcorn stand.

"Right?" I repeated.

He bent down to pick up another rock and wound up; and this time hit the other side of the right-hand boundary picket of that exit fence.

"Aren't you going to answer his question?" Stephen L. asked my brother.

Chris paused then replied, "I already did."

"I didn't hear you say anything," I retorted.

"If they have a fence you won't be able to escape so easily," Chris suggested, brushing the air lightly, with his two peace fingers, toward the space where the nearby fence guarded the border of the amusement park's fantasy with outside reality.

"Oh come on! A little bitty fence like that-

-no problem," I snorted like an aardvark.

"Not if it's a barbed wire fence, or an electric one," Chris cautioned.

"Ooh yeah. I've heard of them. We'd be trapped for sure Mike," Stephen L. worried.

I thought of this. He's right. We'd be cut by barb-wire or electrocuted by electricity. And we really would be stuck in the Midwest. I didn't want to be stuck out there, especially if we couldn't see all the adventures the Midwest had to offer. And I didn't want Stephen L.'s mom to worry. She always gave us Oreo cookies and had let us lick the sugar, scraping the white congealed powder off with our teeth so the cookies would be bare to the black crust. I fixed to think of another adventure. Stephen L. had said he got seasick easily; that meant we couldn't go on any sea cruises. My brother was afraid to fly, so we couldn't do that. I ran out of ideas. So I asked my brother.

"What do you think would be a suitable adventure for us?"

Stephen L. added, "And something that we wouldn't get bored at either."

"We could run a hotel. You'd never get bored about hearing the folks' stories. They'd come from all over and tell you their adventures. And through them you'd have your own picture of what it's like. All in less time than if you had to travel all over the world, say. Plus, you'd be making money while you're doing it."

"That's a great idea Chris!" Stephen L. shouted. "Very knowledgeable. I knew you were smart. Let's do it Mike--a hotel."

"I admit it's a marvelous idea, getting paid and all. But see, we really wouldn't be getting any of those experiences firsthand. I don't want to just look at people's polaroids."

"You could always take a trip," Stephen L. said.

"Yeah, but who would watch the hotel? It takes a lot of people to run one."

Stephen L. said, "No problem. We could alternate while you go on your adventure. Chris and I would watch. Then, I'll go. And you two would stay back at the hotel--and so on. We'd keep switching."

"No. The whole point is to go on the adventure together, the three of us to share it!"

I put my hand in the center and felt the other two hands on top of mine. "Share!" I exclaimed again.

"That's nice you want to share," Chris said, "but with an adventurous lifestyle, we'd be mooching off a lot of people. And the only way we could afford it is if we worked--then took trips together."

"No. No. No good. I made it clear a million times since the first day of the summer--the first day we came through these gates. I made it clear we need to have life like this. An amusement park. When you come to the amusement park--no one works. You only go on different rides and adventures."

"I'm afraid Chris is right Stephen L. I think the hotel idea is the only way to do it."

"But it would mean that we couldn't do it together," I said downtrodden.

I reached into the toybox that Stephen L. had won at the hoop shooting exhibit, and began playing with the dinosaurs, walking the Tyrannasauros Rex into the Stegosaurs' territory.

"Imagine years ago, these big creatures roaming around the desert, ruling everything everywhere they went," Stephen L. said and grabbed the monstrous plant-eating Brontosaurus.

"They went everywhere without worries." I added, moving my T-Rex piece closer to Stephen L.'s large long-necked action figure. "We should be like them. Go wherever we like."

"But we are not big and powerful like they were. We're only kids who wouldn't be able to rule over anything."

I despaired over this and cracked the T-Rex's short arm against the small head of the Brontosaurus, alarming the group.

"A joyful adventure, we could take together for a long time. Maybe it's not about ruling. But we could move around all the time just like them in primitive times, simpler times. And maybe do something like make a career out of it," issued Chris from nowhere, interrupting the captive carnage among the miniature action figures.

"What is it?! I knew you could think of it. You've been spending all this time thinking about it--haven't you?--while we were playing around with these dinosaurs and discussing the options. Ha ha! That's perfect. Now what is it brother?"

"We would become monks--traveling monks…to different cities and countries. This way we wouldn't be married, and not tied down--yet still see everything.

Stephen L. smiled, "Yeah, but that's too strict. We wouldn't be able to have girlfriends."

"I agree with Stephen L.--plus you never

see monks on amusement parks."

"People would think we've gone mad," added Stephen L. sheepishly.

For good measure attempting to further dissuade, "I'm not even sure what monks do, I must confess. It's more serious business than Sunday church-- I know that much. Is this because you've seen Friar Tuck twice?"

Chris answered me, "We wouldn't have as much fun, perhaps, as all the adventures. But we'd be unmarried with freedom and we'd be together," he accentuated the latter with closed palms embraced slowly.

These two topics hit home hard with me-- as hard as my best swing with my thick dark blue Louisville slugger bat. He knew he had me. All I had to do was answer. If I said yes then we would do it. We always agreed that two thirds of the vote carried a majority in our little group; it was mine, Stephen L.'s and Chris's credo. I became nervous. This was a big decision. No wife. No career. No adventure. Well, no adventure as I had envisioned it. But it could be quite an adventure nonetheless. But I didn't know what I was getting into, being a monk. I felt too stupid to ask if he knew exactly what monks did. He must know. Either way, I was caught up in the fantasy of it all. Dreaming of our future was what we did that summer-- whether in the amusement park or playing whiffle-ball in Stephen L.'s backyard, or hiking in the woods at the end of our street.

Chris addressed the fateful question to Stephen L., "What do you say Stephen L?"

Now I got really nervous, almost petrified, by those old woods that the whiffle-ball would often trickle into its brush. Stephen L. had a swaying one third, to align my future with his and my brother's. This was too much for me because unlike with Chris, I could actually see the wheels in Stephen L.'s mind spin, as clear as I could see the merry-go-round. He was about to answer. I grabbed my Oriole cap as Stephen L. was about to answer, and slapped his shoulder with it as a whapped sound whipped against his windbreaker. I always thought it was strange that he covered up his shirtsleeves in summer time. He always felt the need to be cloaked on warm summer days. But he would be warm at night at least. For it was the day before Labor Day and nights could be cool in this Massachusetts suburb where deer roamed the streets at night.

One of us had an idea:

Before we decide let's go to the Pitts.

I anxiously grabbed Stephen L.'s elbow through his nylon jacket to support my won trepidation rather than lead him on.

The Pitts was an enclave, deep in the woods to the west of Stephen L's house. It was a long walk and a difficult trek, even in the daytime. People feared wild bucks and black bears. We would be sojourning at night. As I recall we'd only been there twice. The odds of us getting lost were great I knew, and then perish the thought of running into a bruin.

"Why are we going to the Pitts?" my brother asked.

"All big decisions are made down there. Great struggles by strong men."

"They fight down there," Stephen L. shook his head.

"I know, but they always come out stronger for it."

"They are strong, but not necessarily strong-willed."

"Don't they go hand-in-hand?" I asked.

"Not necessarily," replied Chris.

By this time we had entered the woods. I knew none of us would turn back. No one in our group of three, or the larger group of local kids known as the Deerfield gang, who frequented the Pitts, ever turned around before catching a glimpse of 'The Big Blue Rock.'

Life decisions were made on it, right there in these Pitts. Older kids discussed babies being made there. We didn't know exactly the ramifications of that, but it helped grow the mystique of that Big Blue Rock. And our decision now had every consequence as large as babies being born, at least in our minds. We felt twigs, sticks pierce us and occasionally would stumble on rocks, peeking into the darkness for bruin shapes, with ears attuned to any other rustlings signifying the Pitts' real dangers--close now, we could feel powerful, dark presences. Stephen L.'s flashlight was tiny and dim, and seemed to lose strength every twenty yards or so.

"Shake it," Stephen L.," I encouraged. It glimmered stronger upon the forced movement.

"I think I see it," I urged us on.

Chris squinted, "No. It's not a big enough rock--must be further on." He grabbed the flashlight, moving a few paces ahead of us.

Another football filed was traveled, until Chris spotted 'The Big Blue Rock.' In awe and excitement, Stephen L. fell. I picked him up.

We sat upon it joining Chris now.

All of us felt its power and stolidity. The light shone on several lines of graffiti; it was all over its breadth. These black marks all over it seemed to diminish its power.

"What's that say?" Stephen L. asked pointing very low on the rock, just over a plant, to the only non-dark markings against the old granite.

"Nomad Monks," Chris said and winked. "Let's go home."

He slid the blue crayon he had written it on into his shoe. And we walked after my brother--with no fear a' bruin.

THE END

5 - Today go workah-Tomorrow go workah

Tiller in hand, Dan steered straight but bent over port in the low-riding Lund aluminum boat. He was enjoying the trolling but hadn't looked back at either fishing rod secure in the built-in holders. Heading for the Gulf Stream, his sleek polarized frames were captivated by the lines in the sea. From the depths somehow shot a plant-like green color of tendrils that appeared as laser waves meant to grasp his boat. They were like a spider web splayed out thinly but didn't reach toward the bow in front just near the stern where he studied the lines and the deep blue water beneath it. From sitting on the sea in this low boat, he could feel the ocean, its movements it's tendencies, its light, its darkness, in short its powerful inclinations. Not only that he could sense the current and that what was important when searching for Florida game fish. He owned a depth finder. One afternoon, when he opened the package he thought about using it, but never seriously. He knew he'd rather rely on his fisherman sense. This acuity grew over time. The sea from its depth would send him toward where he needed to be upon due time and relied on due course; the tiller obeyed his hand which obeyed his mind which was attune to the water's attitude of the moment. Some would call it a condition. This, he knew, like the birds were a fleeting pattern at times and a holding one at others. So he would watch birds too. Those who relied solely on the depth finder and the GPS were doomed, he fathomed never to know the joy of fishing quite like he.

"Anna say, she talkja me, I watchum Jeffrey," Ruby apprised me, Dan, as I belched a fried grouper in an ensuing short phone silence before my blast sounded into her ear.

"You watch Jeffrey--tonight?" I asked recovering, clearing the fish frying particles with my tongue.

"After she finished laughing at my excursion, she replied, "Yesum, watchja de Jeffrey."

"What about tomorrow?"

"Mmmm," she pondered and buzzed like a basketball game's twenty-four second clock. "Tomorrow Monday."

I paused and asked in her-speak, "You tomorrow?" meaning, 'So. What about tomorrow?' "I'll cook some dinner. I caught some fish yesterday."

Still an unanswered gap.

"You can prepare your spicy sauce," I enticed.

I thought of how good it would taste and the pleasure of her company, though she always finished her dinner first and slept on the couch from sheer exhaustion. I envisioned myself doing the dishes afterward, content. She would say yes. I could envision it just as I had foreseen my catch after watching the birds too.

"Well?" I asked with an air of happiness and urgency swelling with as much possibility that one in a solitary state of existence could muster.

"Workah!" the blast from this meek speaking Chinese woman, who'd remained silent in all circumstances, curiously enough, even during phone conversations.

We never spoke more than a few lines on the phone. So for my part I speculated that the intuitable gap lie toward reticence rather than reserve. Truthfully and sadly, her response and my interpretation of it, was as predictable as waterways leading to the ocean.

I decided to put an end to the conversation in one of my usual manners, inevitably an occasion to drone but at other moment remain more optimistic. I didn't know where my tone lay then as I hung up the receiver after having issued, yet again,

"Call me when you have time."

She had already repeated my sentiment; except when Ruby's translation imported, "When I time--I give you a car."

"I'm driver," she added in a hurried tone. She never hung up right away but I figured she must always put the phone down on the passenger side seat, as sometimes I'd plead,

"Wait," to try to find out her schedule when I damn well knew what it was--booked solid with work or babysitting or some other business networking endeavor.

The most time we spent together was when I taught her to drive at Haulover Park. Not having any kids of my own, it made me feel good to teach someone such a skill. She drove so slow in the beginning with a fear that lessened as usual over time.

There's that word again. Time. That evil, over-the-shoulder word. How could it produce such rancor within me? It's my birthright. When you're a Capricorn you feel like you should scale a mountain in one bound. And you expect the same of others when they're on board, on your shift, or preparing something for you in the kitchen. Then when it's all complete: the driving lesson, the work shift, or the dinner, there is always the fail-safe, same excuse.

'I'm tired--have to be up early.'

As much as I hated the quick phone hello-goodbyes and the feelings of abandonment it left me with, it pissed me off far less than not even giving me a shot, a chance to see me, to spend some time together, no matter how brief. And that was the case now when she uttered, "Workah!" I went into a rage. Why? I was broke. But that wasn't the only reason. The main reason is I can't take working for someone and having someone correct me. Correction--I can't take working for ANYONE. So I shredded the want ads in a million pieces. I turned the blower of the large oscillating fan on in the bedroom and blew them through my bedroom door into the living room.

Anna called the next night.

"I need you to watch my Jeffrey."

"When?" I curled a scrap of want ad under my toes; the shreddings piled up dropping at an angle onto the green chair leg at my kitchen table. I grabbed the remainder of the paper and slammed it into the waste bucket.

"Maybe 12:30 to 3:30 on Saturday."

Great. Right in the middle of the afternoon--not enough time to start fun activities: swimming, boating, fishing, running; only enough time to make confession before 4:30 mass. But I hadn't any plans and could not think of an idle excuse so I agreed to sit.

Ruby called the night after I sat as she always did when I completed the favor. I never understood if it was a promise to see me when she 'had time' or if it was benevolent Chinese courtesy borne out of custom. The courtesy call was appreciated but it was wearing as thin as the ink levels on a cutting edge printer whose cartridge couldn't detect and tell the operator the acuity of just how low the levels were preceding a faded print on the page.

Friday night the phone rang. It was Ilvania, a twenty one year old hottie who I met on the set of a Spanish soap on Thursday. She designed her own dresses, which she had sold to Bennifer. She was loaded. I'd been forty-five minutes early and she and her mom, who was visiting Ilvania from El Salvador stepped out of their Mercedes (SUV). I was the only gringo at breakfast and ate alone. She seemed impressed later in the morning when we talked, on the shuttle heading toward the shoot's set, of my book tour and interviews I'd done. I gawked longer than anyone else both times she stepped into a new homemade dress. A triangular green number which gave new meaning to my take on the newly minted term 'Fush Buck' a pointed symbol to her groin region, exposing her flanks, full bodied, but not busty. And those eyes! Green eyes set catlike above an ultra strong wide jaw. Huge lips. She had given me several flirty looks while at the top of the shopping aisle where cameras rolled and one large mobile in the center of our aisle was almost sitting riding up my and Ilvania's mother's butts, separating us; we were holding on either side of the camera the handles on a single grocery cart, filled with miscellaneous Spanish sodas and chips, Ilvania being a dozen feet away. The mom spoke broken English.

"You just have to tell her four times," Ilvania laughed at lunch break later when I'd asked her mother where the dessert was served.

Mom all but offered her daughter to me when I told her I had a boat.

"Maybe you go...here...over there...all the way with Ilvania...on the boat.

'Ya' I thought on the ride home looking at the business card Ilvania gave me after I gave her mine too. I hadn't noticed until now that she'd done the modeling for the three pictures on one side. The end two, being color shots the middle a black and white. The one on the left was perhaps the sexiest shot, a white top hat over her, hmm natural brown eyes with right elbow resting on her left wrist as the left hugged snugly her hot pink bikini. Long blond hair, splayed over her left shoulder, and striped down her tanned bustline underneath her left forearm. Her arms formed an L for the viewer. Her fingers gracefully held the brim of her hat while pinky and thumb in the foreground gave it an extra suave look. The picture on the right displayed her in a blue miniskirt holding matching coverall behind her. Strapped matching heels with high guards near her shin gave captured her as a runway model, for she appeared to be standing on the edge of a divingboard, which somehow matched her outfit. She looked particularly vulnerable and matadoorish, skinnier too, as her six pack showed. The middle photograph was the answer to the cover shot lifting bug-eyed shades over her right eye. The matching black and white photo in front showed an ultra up-close look at the divas flawless face. Lips parted more. The shades had sparkles, which attempted to hide her dark sultry eyes. The eyebrows appeared as a great continuous wave, set finely tracing without any gap, upon the upper rim of the oversized glasses, which matched her hoop size earrings. She looked topless though she wasn't; the definition of her neck and upper chest gave a mystique as to what cup size she boast. Ilvania said she could be found at her sister's store, for which this modeling session promoted, on Friday's and Saturdays.

    I was just about to call Ruby when sure enough the phone rang.

    "Hi Dan," I was wondering if you want

to go out on the boat some time."

"Sure. When?" Damn. I knew I shouldn't have left planning in her hands.

"How about?" she gleamed and swept a laser like ray of green beaming across her visage then parked them wide-eyed right into my view, as I imagined on with delight into the finite frays of those green lanterns held up to my face, flushing color into my head as I recognized perspiration pushing betwixt my brows. She had thick brows and long lashes as I wore equally as well. I broke off the imaginary gaze whereupon her white nail polish on hands stretched out on each lap in my mind.

Ruby rushed through the traffic as best she could. Her boss berated her but she couldn't understand the brunt off the message just the tone. She tried not to let it bother her. And it didn't. What did bother her was working all day hoping for customers to come into the nail shop. The old women, regulars who'd come in the past few months, never tipped well, if at all. Ruby didn't know how she would pay Anna rent this month. So frustrating not being able to save money. She wanted to buy her own condo. And the car was always breaking down. How many favors could she call on and how many times would she be in debt to others? This wasn't what she expected when she opted to come from China to the land of opportunity. The door jingled. The customer made a beeline for her, walking right past Ruby's wide smile to the other hairdresser who normally cut the woman's hair as well as her nails. Ruby dropped her long black hair and eyes peered up at the facial section. She was optimistic that the next customer would be for a facial and she would land her. That would be nearly as much money as the co-worker would make and in less time too. If only the jingle would ring some one else in.

No one came into the beauty salon until the next day. A girl who dwarfed the slight Ruby. Ruby knew the type. A high flyer who'd obviously had her hair done down by Lincoln Road and a facial off Decco Drive. She just wanted to touch up her nails here.

They were white.

The girl started to complain, "I chipped them while fishing on a boat."

Ruby smiled for she happened to understand the sentence in its entirety; oftentimes the greetings of customers baffled her. But Ruby knew what the client needed and what led up to the young woman's problem.

Ruby worked diligently and after responding to the girl asked in turn, "You go bow?" The girl, rightly inferring boat as the correct point of the question, had nodded while Ruby held the scissors in suspension high atop her dyed blond hair. Though it was boring watching Ilvania's tired look, Ruby was grateful, for the young woman tipped her well. She watched her hop into the Mercedes SUV and Ruby wondered how many nails she'd have to clip to drive something like that.

Dan weighed his options. Keep calling Ruby or call Ilvania back for another date. He hadn't dated for a year or so. He lost track of it really. There were too many gold-diggers down here to bother with. Ilvania already had money. Ruby had nothing. Dan had nothing. One path was paved with toil and struggle the other rode high with flash and promise.

They both had good hearts. Both were fun. One had plenty of time. The other was booked. One had family obligations, the other a parent in a different hemisphere. One called him constantly of late, the other picked up the phone only to answer his numerous inquiries. One was months older than he, the other much younger. He had connubial aspirations while it appeared marriage may well be the last bastion in either of their minds.

How much longer? And he hadn't even started dating yet. He yearned for the Gulf Stream; those tendrils sprung up from the deep would steer that course for him eventually.

THE END

6 - Boat Won't Work

"Justin Brant has the best boat in the whole Miami Beach Marina," the boat clerk sang out gleefully as I paid him cash to get the boat back in operation.

I'm unsure when I began to believe that proclamation, after having actually attempted to sell it; the eighth cardinal sin in my estimation. But I do know when I absolutely believed it. Memorial Day weekend. And it's not even Memorial Day yet as I begin to write of this perhaps miraculous event. Before I commence to tell you what gave rise to concurring with the clerk, let me give you the lowdown on this low riding boat.

It's history, the Cincinnati--neither a she nor a he, but it's been my baby in that I'm attached to it like a single mom is to her adored only child. I don't brush its teeth or change its diapers, but in a sense I do. For instance, I scrape the barnacles off about once every season, the latest being just Friday afternoon kicking off the holiday weekend. Of course, in Florida we only have two seasons, winter and summer.

Notwithstanding, the Lund was bought at a boat show in Providence, cheaper than Boston's, so I got a better deal. Or so I thought. Remember the old adage?--you get what you pay for...Well, okay--I'll try to stay positive.

Most people received a car for graduation. I made out better, in my mind, because I got a boat albeit years later.

As my dad and I haggled with the salesman, or technically the distributor, in the Dedham Massachusetts' cellar office, Larry tried selling us on the larger model with a steering wheel. I felt lucky to be getting a boat so I didn't push.

Surprisingly, I heard myself say, "I think I prefer the tiller-operated one."

"The small one? It's only 15 ½ feet," Brian the other salesman pitched.

Now I paused because I liked its blue color. But hell, I oughta have one closer to 17 foot--so the 16 ½ hunter green Lund became the one for me.

"This one," I said definitively.

"You're sure now? You can have the one with the steering wheel," my dad assured.

"Naw," I replied, "you had pretty good luck dad with the ole Hunky Dory and that was a tiller too, a half foot smaller. And this one weights less too. So it oughta be easy to trailer-- me being one person trekin' to Florida and all."

"You're going to Florida?" Brian grinned. Getting out of this cold--good for you. What are you going to do down there?"

"Fishing charters." I told him my dreams as I told everyone. My dad got antsy to pay for it with his checkbook out. So I gave a condensed version and we were on the road home ten minutes later.

On the ride home, I thought of my history with boats. It started on my Uncle Pinky's boat. We fished for Tautog, just a few football fields short of Cleveland's Ledge--a lighthouse in the middle of Buzzards Bay, between Mattapoisett and West Falmouth. To the east, we'd see resident birds forever flocking around Bird Island. The railroad bridge was visible behind that. We anchored and observed how fearless Uncle Pinky performed in baiting our hooks with seaworms, their dangerous black snappers protruding; they resembled Captain's hook gaffed hand.

"What else do Tautog like to eat?" asked my brother.

"These." Pinky answered with a smile and an ever-present accompanying grunt. He had reached in the new 18 foot boat's glistening white live well and pulled out a paper bag holding wet dark green crabs that menacingly shot their claws close to our peeking faces exposed over the bag. These creatures made the seaworms appear harmless.

"How's the boat running?" my dad asked Pinky.

"Good. It's damn new. It better run well seeing how it's only in its second season."

My brother Dougie and I suppressed a laugh upon Pinky's pet expression, 'damn new.' We wondered if he meant brand new, but recalled he'd said this before about the Seven T's, which stood for Trainor, his last name. And I thought it was strange that none of his offspring ever fished with him. More room for us; I never brought that to the surface at Aunt Mary's dinner table.

"Who wants to bait these nasty critters?"

Pinky inquired.

We cowered as we studied his lobster-like face. It appeared as if he always had a sunburn; tough to know by complexion alone for our fishing expeditions never began until August, hence the near retiring fisherman took us out on the Seven T's. Usually, we'd catch rock bass, which we were thrilled with until we witnessed Pinky catch a four pound Tautog a few weeks later toward the end of last season.

That winter after the Seven T's second season, my brother Dougie and I talked incessantly about fishing and needing a boat until my father finally relented. Did that mean we could get out and anchor next to Pinky by Cleveland's Ledge?

No. Not on a teacher's salary, my dad briefed. But we were able to get out on the water. And what we eventually discovered when we plunked ourselves in our blue, used, chipped-out, splinters-up-the ass interior was even better than Tautog. For now we fished closer in for...Bluefish; in the spring and fall--they were absent every summer, which was okay I guess because we wouldn't have wanted to get up at 5 a.m. every day. The great secret about Bluefishing too, we learned, with our own personal tutor, Paul, who had inherited these skills from his mom--a real pro, Satchi, was that unfathomably you didn't need bait nor lures.

Satchi's mom had told ours that Paul's first Bluefish was caught from the shore when he was only three years old. So this was a real pro. Plus, he was a resident here, not just a summer person. So he knew how to catch them here at Aucoot Cove, though he didn't say much at first that summer. And I never could solve how he could simply stare at the water and know exactly where the Bluefish schools were located. But every time we went with him, we caught bluefish--if there were any to be caught. We never used bait on the schools of Bluefish we'd encounter. No, we fooled'em with a hook. Well, three hooks to be accurate--oversized treble hooks. Paul showed me and my brother along with Myatt, the other neighborhood summer chum that often accompanied our expeditions--how to jerk the hook through the school to 'snag a pogie.'

'Didja snag one?' one could hear one little rowboat beckon to the other on these still Aucoot Cove misty mornings. Paul showed us how to wait and let it sink. Count to five or six, or more, he'd say. We did. And it seemed like the number should have been higher. It took us a couple seasons to figure this out, as Paul, alone in his boat often responded affirmatively to that, 'Didja snag one?' question moreso than anyone else. In fact, I don't think he ever asked the question. Paul was just too busy reading the water or the sky. He'd spot feeding birds looking desperately for prey in the ocean as if he were the one that hadn't fed.

For a few years we had our fun in the blue rowboat until dad paid for 'The Hunky Dory.' I was fifteen then. It was great to bottom fish, but Tautog with thick lips and rounded caudal fin seemed to be around only late in the season--very long in the tooth for anglers awaiting the brown fishes feeding time, which the species did primarily in the fall, with their human-like molars to crush crabs. In the boats first few years, dad always took it out of the cove to winterize it much too early; though now with a motorized boat, we figured we had it made for blue fishing-- no need to row harder, chasing the fast moving schools around the heavier breakers by Converse Point, the peninsula, which was dotted with a helipad landing at the mansion;

the point's edge enclosing ritzy Marion Harbor's western border. Now with the Hunky we'd be able to zoom after the Chopper-Blues.

Boy, were we wrong. Even though we only had a 25 horse-power engine, it spooked those bluefish schools so that they'd dive downward and we could no longer spot the school never mind snag a pogie. Maneuvering The Hunky into position in order to cast into the center of a school was no easy task. On the occasion that we were able to accomplish this effect, the physical snagging was a problem. Due to the fact the sides of our Hunky were higher, the angle of the line would be raised too high and the hook would sail over the pogies' dorsals. So we'd snag air violently and nearly fall like a baseball player missing after a big home run swing a la Reggie Jackson's corkscrew cleats-shins-knees-and thighs, whiffs. Frustration brewed since all we caught were the smallish snapper blues in this manner. Paul landed all the big'uns and a squeteague; this sea trout species inhabiting the very bottom of the school. They were less aggressive so trailed behind for the scraps when the blues would annihilate the pogies. Paul kept saying the noise scared the fish; so we couldn't fish at the same school as his. He said that shouldn't be a problem because we could zoom all over Aucoot Cove and Marion Harbor to find the schools. But it seemed like the schools closest to shore held the biggest fish. That was obvious to us by gauging the size later in the morning at Paul's filet station on his porch. Lesson being in all of this--it pays to keep it simple!

And I suppose that's why I chose the Lund model that I did; tiller meant more work, less leisure involved, yet...simpler.

The name Cincinnati trotted to the forefront of my mind for the Lund perhaps through a conduit of history, honoring a legendary general --U.S. Grant, the cigar smoking general. As I sat on my condo porch in a suburb southwest of Boston, I stared into the woods smoking a stogie, rationalizing how Grant being an outstanding calvalryman at the outset of the war, rode Cincinnati, his warhorse to victory after victory in the Civil War battles; and he parlayed that into two presidential terms. Powerful stuff--I figured my boat with such a name, would be a favorite in the marina and amongst customers in Miami Beach. Cincinnati would be a conduit of annals hereupon, to whatever stardom, imparted by my namesake, hoofed and spawned on to me from the ages.

After watching my smoke rings puff and thin into the woods, I turned the end of the cigar toward me and studied the ashes directly after my next inhalation--the orange behind the razory dark black ashes. That's it! I'll have each letter of the word Cincinnati resemble a cigar ash illumination. It was, however, tricky explaining this to the people who designed the logo; yet it came out smoking. The only defect in the delivery was that I wanted a horse with five general's stars surrounding the horse. The gold stars came out fine, but the gold horse possessed no visible mane or tail as the workers made those parts dark brown; a color that does not gallop to one's eye well particularly on a hunter green paint job.

Anyways, it was berthed in the waters of Lake Massapoag in Sharon Massachusetts.

'Pull it. Pull it. Try it again. The choke. Pull it--no no, you must've flooded it,' remonstrated dad animatedly'

On the idle pond, the hapless verbal suggestions went on for hours. My brother and dad watched my strenuous efforts, in vain. I tried to stay positive, but I swore. Then I drove my fist into the side green, felt paneling, which covered the livewell. I was sweating bullets and it was a cool May afternoon now turned evening. It didn't work. I couldn't believe it. It was...DAMN NEW-- and it didn't work. My heart felt gelid and as hexed as an Indian severed from his land by shrewd white man's legal maneuverings.

"We're taking this back," I told my dad.

"No. Let's call Brian--see what he has to say."

Brian was out of the office. Larry was out of the office. It was July before we met with them. We trailered it down and Brian made some adjustments.

"What was the problem?" we asked him.

"Nothing. It must be that you played with the idle dial. See how it turns on the throttle," he demonstrated.

I tried to remember. To start it, it did seem like we moved every knob and dial hour after hour to make it go."

"What did it sound like?" asked Brian.

"It sounded good at first," I answered, "then right before I put it in forward gear, it stalled and we couldn't start it back up."

"Well, try again. I'm sure you'll have no

problem--it's a new engine. No one ever usually has a problem with this brand of new motors."

This time Dougie and I plied Lake Sabbatia in Taunton, a ten minute jaunt from Sharon. The boat ramp was crowded. We finally backed the car, trailer, and boat up, wedging them through the narrow space. We unwound The Hunky from winch, as the wind and current made our legs unsteady. The rocky pavement underneath was slick with algae. We disembarked and paddled a good distance, making our way clear of the boats clogging up the ramp area. The sun was out. I smiled at my brother, tried to relax and said, "Here we go." I pulled and...music to our ears, the motor turned over loudly. On the tiller, I revved it once, twice. Doug opened the hatch to put the oars away, as he'd been paddling hard to stem the tide and keep our course from drifting to the leeward island in the large pond. Just as the compartment slammed shut, we heard a sputter.

"No!" I groaned.

"Give it more gas," Doug instructed.

"Shit."

It was too late. Needless to say, Cincinatti

didn't start again that day. The third time was a charm. From subsequent trips on out, it was hit or miss. One time okay--next time, no-go. More phone calls to Brian. Some good explanations of what it could be, but nothing substantial for the execution of his instructions because the adjustments weren't always translatable into a positive administering of engine start up.

I tried not to invite friends on board for embarrassment of the boat not working. That winter I decided to take a captain's license course. I thought I might learn a thing or two. Some one in class was bound to have the same boat, or at least similar problems to what I'd experienced with my new boat.

I was wrong. Oh well. I looked forward to the final test with my plotters and slide rule in hand. As I waited in line for the test results, some people were high-fiving. I knew how good this would feel. I'd be able to do charters this year in Boston before moving to Florida the following year--a year's experience would help. I'd done canoe charters for a couple years, but on the motorboat would give me more credibility to potential customers I figured. They showed me the score, 65 in red. Seventy was passing.

"You need to work on your plotting," is what they told me.

My father and brother encouraged me to take it again. But I knew I couldn't--not with those maps they required us to plot on--the Vineyard and its objects in necessary ranges. I couldn't relatively think of that island or its surrounding lines of positions through points without feeling as perilous as a mariner without a compass or pelorus. For I had a love that went awry on the island--very awry. And I simply could not think of that place and not get down. I knew if the tests had those Vineyard maps, I'd never be successful in taking the test again in Massachusetts. Florida was my correct answer. I knew that without a doubt now through that failure.

When I was trying to find a place to live in Florida, I fought hard to have the company also ship my canoe inside the Lund. There was a risk it might damage the boat. I'll take that risk. However, I had no pull as my dad intervened countering strongly. And since he was the one writing the check to the mover, the canoe would not make the journey, not to Florida at least. For dad sold it to cousin Paul whose kids would enjoy it on the lake by their house on Boston's north shore.

I met the man who delivered it at Haulover Marina in Miami Beach. The older black gentleman was taking pictures of the mangroves as the sun set when I addressed him.

"Everything go okay?" I asked.

"Sure--only problem was a box or two fell out back a ways."

"Oh," I said. What was in it?"

"Don't know. I didn't check the insides of the boxes. They were closed up with tape. Was it anything valuable?"

"I don't know," I answered, " I'll need to check the other boxes first."

We walked over to the boat and as he told me he'd like to take my dad out fishing up north in his own boat, my heart sank, as it was my brand new fish-finder that had toppled over, somewhere on Route 95 in Virginia, he thought.

"Did you stop anywhere?" I was still holding out hope that if he'd stopped--maybe he'd left the boxes at a motel somewhere and we could call.

"No. I drove all the way through," he said proudly. "I've got another delivery to pick up in North Carolina soon--got to move. See ya--enjoy your boat!"

That's stupid. No wonder he lost it. He

was rushing. I tried to manage a smile and a brief wave and thought of all the companies that trailer boats; we had to pick him. I couldn't help but think that if the canoe were there, none of this would have happened. And I'd have the damned canoe.

I was more flurried the day the Cincinatti put in, in Florida. After the bottom was painted black at Maule Marina on Biscayne Boulevard, I finally corralled my drinking buddy Riccardi, a large Puerto Rican, cabbage-patched doll character who used to be loaded. Riccardi had had his own businesses, but now stole his groceries every week across the street from the low-rent motel where he resided. He knew everything about cars and boats, especially motors. Erewhile, he assured me he could fix whatever was wrong with mine; and with his motor-mouth this could be a white lie.

As I wrote the check at the cashier's desk, I peeked through the window and could see him pulling the crank for all he was worth.

I walked outside issuing to Riccardi, "I warned you. Didn't I?" as the engine made nary a glurgle.

He returned, "Don't worry. I've got it. Just give me a minute."

One minute turned into thirty, which inched to forty-five long minutes.

"I gotta use the bathroom." I walked across the street to the gas station to get as far away as possible, for now, from the…fatuity of it all.

When I returned Riccardi enthused, "Where you been man? I got it started right after you left. Come on."

"How did you do it?" I was incredulous to learn. I shouted the same question again over the purring motor.

He replied, "I just took my time. Patience."

"No. I mean the choke. How many times did you pull it? Was it all the way out? Or…"

"I don't know."

"Try to remember."

"I tinkered with it. It's too bad you weren't here to watch me."

I paid him in Coronas as I promised the thirsty, sweaty Riccardi. Then we discussed him helping me put whips in next week with more Coronas in his future.

Once the whips were installed, it took a week or two before I learned how much the tide rose and dropped so I could keep the boat far enough off the seawall. But in that time the port side became damaged so that the green lettering 'Lund Rebel' was scraped off, as well as intermittent blotches along the same flank.

These aesthetics never bothered me fraught with my own fatwittedness. The motor however is another story.

The Cincinatti stranded me three or four times in the intracoastal. In retrospect, Sea Tow gold card was my best purchase, even more than my insurance, which thankfully I never had to use. Every time it was towed to Sunny Isles Marina, where their employees were always happy to give it a few joy rides, inevitably.

The first time I had it repaired I became angry when Brandon summarized what went wrong. 'Mr. Grant...this...Mr. Grant...that.'

I immediately accused, "You guys didn't even fix the livewell."

He sighed mightily which exacerbated me even more, "It worked when we tried it here."

Each time I paid him and his alternating smug and sympathetic looks, which worked well enough for me to oftentimes pay twice or thrice for what to me was essentially a prior problem that never became wholly repaired.

Each time I swore to myself they'd never rook me and would demand better explanations of their repairs. Each time I felt like a loser, a sucker, a fool on both of these counts.

At least I've got 'the best boat in the marina.'

I heard that oxymoron from some one every time. The owner went so far to say that he'd buy it if he had the money. How can you not have the dough with all the checks I wrote you?

The heart wrenching backbreaker was the following episode... I guess this occurred around the halfway point of the numerous repairs to the Cincinnati:

Responding to Brandon's, "It worked when we tried it here..." Justin replied,

"Damn, I just put a down payment on a ring for my girl, and you guys are really cutting into my next few installments."

"Boats are a lot of maintenance. This really isn't that bad. You should see the bills that some of these other guys have-- thousands of dollars," he swept his arm and his eyes followed skyward in a grand gesture meant to ease my blow. "You got off easy. Plus, your girl must know that every fisherman is married to his boat."

He bit on his lower lip while gripping the counter and staring hard at me, apparently waiting for confirmation, which I now gave him.

"My girlfriend barely speaks English."

"Well, she'll know that to be true when you're out all day chasing Mahi-mahi instead of mowing the lawn."

"You know that saying--the two best days a boat owner has are the day he buys a boat, and the day he sells it? Well fellas," another boat mechanic gazed over the conversation, sipping a small coffee through the lid, wiping it off his dark full bottom lip as he reached for a honey glaze donut, "I am beginning to think some weight is attached to that statement."

"Nah. Everyone says the same. But if they really believed it, there'd be a lot more dock space here in South Florida. You can bet on that boss."

"So it worked when you tried it here. We'll be happy to look at it again."

"I held up my hand. Don't worry. If costs are involved, I'll just manually bucket the water into it myself."

"Suit yourself," he smiled as I whipped out my checkbook, he added, "Out of curiosity what cut of diamond did you choose?"

"I didn't."

"It's not a bubblegum ring is it?" The laughter from the back room reached me; the yellow capped chap coughing off his guffaw, in back nearly blew donut crumbs clear into the back of Brandon's head.

"It's a Colombian ring, no points. It has an emerald."

"Well, that's different." It was tough to tell if he was impressed or sympathetic.

"Yes it is. See you guys later…I'm sure."

I had made several trips to the Wyndham Miami Beach. Every time I valet-parked which was once a month to make my payments, the valet after my instructions not to roll my window down would inevitably, upon my waiting for my Camry's return, see it being driven as it rolled to the pick up area, with no surprise, yet again the window down. I tipped him in spite of my burning desire to call him a very fine idiot indeed. The automatic switch to roll it up would not work; somehow it was on about a fifteen minute power delay, so more than half my ride back home would be spent in extreme heat. And in those days of threatening skies, I'd have the fear of getting soaked; the latter occurring once.

This particular day, I was excited. I was on my halfway payment and had long decided that after this payment I would ask Sherry to marry me. The prior time I had reminded them to fit the ring to the size of one of the female employees who worked at the gift shop, near the jewelry shop in the court's exclusive hotel. She had looked as if she had the same size fingers. The woman upon my request showed me proudly the ring. I looked at it, smiled...then immediately frowned.

"This hasn't been sized. Your man didn't reduce the size. We said size 6 ½."

"Yes," the Colombian woman said as if everything were in order.

"Why is it still the same size as before?"

With my demeanor and octave increased, she was beginning to sense my perturbance.

"I know. The theeng is--he does not size."

"Wait a minute. You told me he does size. You told me you were going to ship it off and he'd do it...free of charge. That was our negotiation." I waited for an explanation from the smiling, quaint and quite innocent woman of a still nature that belied my extreme incredulity.

"Yes."

"What do you mean yes?! I shouted.

She looked nervous, then her glance found the phone. "Hmm, excuse me sir. Let me call. I no understand."

I waited and waited and waited.

"Sorry sir--she is transferring me. I want to know what happened so I can tell you."

She smiled as the person on the line informed her of the ring's plight.

I felt bad news was imminent, but held out hope for the Colombian woman was still smiling.

"Yes. Sir we do not fit the ring. Okay. Nothing we can do. We have other rings that I can show you, or you can take this one and have some one else fit it."

"No. You've been collecting my payments and I don't want another ring. Listen, you told me you'd fit that ring so I want it fitted. Let me talk to your boss."

"No sir. The problem is thaaht this ring cannot be fitted. The stone would come out. It's delicate. No way they can do."

"Fine. Let me have the money back."

As she counted the bills, the only consolation I found was the knowledge that I could put this money into the breakdown that my boat endures, though my heart be crushed with this setback to my course toward a marriage procession.

After a few breakdowns later, (me and the boat), coupled with the marina's substantially raised labor, I decided to sell it. Being unemployed for a few months, I figured I'd need to sell it in order to eat. So I advertised in Boat Trader magazine. A guy called. He offered me less than half the blue-book. Get real. Maybe I should've accepted the offer; I reviewed many nights. Maybe my brother had been right--that a boat only sells for half of its value. Not this boat. Not my Cincinnati. I'd protect it through thick and thin. Heck, I was still eating. And I hadn't stolen any groceries either. But according to my brother, I had more serious transgressions to concern myself with...

...It started at the doorway. That's where the demons congregated. We had returned from downtown Miami after I had been cited for a parking ticket. I'd been job hunting and my brother was along. I raged out about the ticket at my condo kitchen door--and how dumb the cop was for I had even asked the policeman if it was alright to park in that spot. When we returned home I kept complaining about the parking ticket and how I couldn't find a job, or a girlfriend that spoke English down here--all the frustrations major and minor flowed out. I received a phone call from my Chinese girlfriend who brought over young Jeffrey for me to watch. I took out the trash, slammed the door, yelled, "Fuck," opened the garbage chute, slammed it with another expletive, came in and bitched about the plumbing bill, the neighbors, the boat again; then an argument ensued with my brother about my 'not being anywhere near ready for marriage.'

I deigned to reach the kitchen door to rush away brushing by him, muttering aloud,

"Why's it always me? Shit." The door had locked remaining jammed. "Uuuugghh!! And now…WHAT THE FUCK!!"

"You want to know why?"

He seemed sincere. And I thought it strange that he took my rhetorical rantings for an inquisition begging a retort.

"Ya!" I snapped.

"Because…" clasping his hands together, "Say a prayer with me?"

I wanted to rebel against the request, but something deep in me couldn't.

I acquiesced and we said a quick one-- either Hail Mary or Our Father; I don't remember which. But then he said it; something that would change my course in more ways than one forever.

"You have demons of rage attached to you."

After suppressing a desire to slam a cabinet or laugh, I questioned, "How can you say that after having been with me so short a period of time?"

"Well." He paused as he always tended to judiciously do, but this pause bothered me much more than the sum of all previous interludes. He continued, "Based on this afternoon…"

"You're basing…saying I have demons of rage attached to me because I flipped out over a ticket. Is that all? It's normal anger."

"If you continue with illicit relations with Sherry, you're going to have nothing but continued trouble." He pointed to the lock as exhibit Z.

I fashioned the illustration unbelievably absurd and totally disconnected.

Until.

One evening I returned home, after having consistently for a full week attended daily Mass as a repentance for Lenten Observance at the season's advent. This was three weeks after his troubling visit, which intruded upon my soul, treading slowly yet surely. I tried the kitchen door lock--the one that didn't budge before. Normally, I used the other door, but before I even realized what door I was at--I had the kitchen door *open*. Whoa! Wait a minute. Could he have been right? When he left Florida the boat had started after a long layoff, resting in sick bay against my seawall slot. And we did fish in the bay. The motor was very rough sounding. He caught a small grunt. He was thrilled because we saw a manatee. The sun set and I resigned myself to the fact that this meager fish would be the last one ever caught aboard the Cincinnati.

I completed my Lenten observance of daily early morning church, grinding it out, weighing religion against the societal tide that threatened to wash over me every waking moment. And my chastity continued for well over forty days as well. As the weeks passed by, my Chinese girlfriend, Sherry, went by the wayside with her work obligations and plans to go to New York at some point. I was still optimistic to marry her until…

Twilight--Sherry's sister Myra called up out of the blue, "Justin--do you mind watching my Jeffrey?"

"No of course not." I always helped when I could. "Where's Sherry? She usually watches him."

"She is here with me; and you know Sherry's friend too, from Detroy."

"Yeah. I know she has a visitor from Detroit. Where are you?"

"We're watching…at the place--where the girls take off their clothes."

"You're at a strip joint. Why are you watching girls?"

"No--men."

"Oh" I knew now. It was La Bear night club next to Solid Gold. La Bear being beefcake. Solid Gold, cheesecake.

"Why don't you come join us?" Sherry's sister asked innocently enough.

For beefcake or cheesecake? Both made

me nervous considering my new life path of purity. I didn't think it was a good idea to be in the vicinity of either appetizer. But my palette must've been whetted for I went. When I made it to the parking lot Sherry could tell how pissed I was. But I held it together...somewhat for Jeffrey's sake. Myra came and gave Sherry some money--tip money for the guys. I was steaming. I could use this money to fix my boat. Our collective agreement was to help one another out financially, or, other simpler every day challenges. Sherry is out of work too and hurting as bad as I am for money; and here she is giving money freely to men she didn't even know. Boy that pisses me off.

So it wasn't too hard to call Denise my co-worker when she wrote her number down next Friday afternoon at work. By Saturday Denise had directions to my place and arrived there with her son Jason. She walked in the door smiling, aglow under a wide-brimmed, cosmopolitan blue hat--complete with tight jeans and blue tank top hugging her Jamaican sway in place as she sashayed breezily into the room with a white drench-coat sheen of lip gloss cohered against light-toned, ebony, fleshy lips that glistened somehow beneath the hat's shade.

Cruising through Haulover Inlet's soft waves, which ruffled her Dramamine feathers, for the swells were high in her estimation. I was shocked when she said,

"I'm going to kill you Justin. I'm going to kill you." She kept laughing and repeating my death.

"But who'd drive?" My reply put an end to her laughter and my threatened demise.

The day was blazing sun--a blessing on Memorial Day weekend--a Saturday.

The first stop, just offshore, we didn't catch a thing. Denise sampled a shrimp. A shrimp platter that I'd bought--not the fish's fare, hard shelled ones that I purchased from Tarpon Tackle. She became nauseous. I never carried Dramamine and Denise had nothing for seasickness either. However, she recovered in time to catch a Spanish Mackerel. Then a grunt. Then la crème de la crème--a Yellowtail Snapper. When it reached the boat, little fleckings of plankton, iridescently immersed, thickly in the pale, mint-green surface water, crisply framing the yellowtail, now holding parallel, tight to the line--about to brush the surface, no longer scutting, but gliding effortlessly, pulled steadily alongside the boat by myself as Denise had handed me the rod halfway through the run. With the sun hung high reflecting off the white-brimmed World Sportsman hat, I was poised for the swift hoist aboard and felt at one with everything, not thinking about anything at all but the splendor of the serene scene.

The sun shone glinting rays, kissing the fish's yellow bars.

I leaned over to unhook it. "Yellowtails have small mouths so they can be difficult to catch. Fisherman's success depends on what hook size one chooses. "

"I guess you chose the right one," Denise said.

As Denise edged closer the snapper I'd been holding out of the water for too long a time, awestruck by its beauty were we; the blue-brim cast a necessary shade over the bright yellowness of the fish's flank as I threw it into the live well.

"Thank you for cleaning the barnacles," she added. Her eyes traced the yellow snapper's deep yellow stripe, which extended all the way from it snout to caudal fin; it swam cheerfully in the limited live well space.

Then Denise kissed me on the cheek as

thin Jason grinned harmoniously out of his orange lycra muscle shirt at the fish, the yellowtail and the Spanish Mackerel, side by side; the grunt we threw back. Jason then peered openly, making eye contact with the yellowtail's red eye; those fish were separated by a black divider in the livewell.

Funny. As I pulled the plug to drain the water that I'd manually bucketed in to fill the well for the baitfish and shrimp, I thought of this now unplumbed event on this blessed weekend--the livewell was the only thing about that boat that didn't work.

Brandon and the boys were right. It was the best boat after all.

THE END

7 - Fire Extinguishers

I walked into the shower and locked eyes with a black man, ripped with muscle, no fat on him; the prototype for a fireman if I ever saw one. The sizing up was not however in a challenging (sense) for he was a new acquaintance of mine already. His name is DeRose. My eyes didn't leave his. He was biting his lip and on the verge of a breakdown. He'd been crying. I saw the tears and wondered what I could say to help him. Within the first second or two, it was at that particular moment that I might be considered in his eyes another callous white intruder, especially at such a vulnerable place as a shower with nothing but a bar of white soap resting along his large black fingers, as well as a distance of possibly three yards. I'd forgotten my soap and was about to ask to borrow his at that awkward moment of two naked men looking at each other in the shower, but neither on under any running water. I couldn't be that callous and leave him in tears so I decided to do the decent, compassionate thing.

"What's wrong?" I gently inquired.

Would he act defensive, nervous, tense? I broke through--the tone was right and the eye contact convinced him. He'd been in the shower, but just standing there without a towel. Maybe DeRose intended to air dry, but it appeared there would not be enough time for that given two reasons, first this man's girth; secondly, the militant trainers at the Fire Academy allowed us 'ten minutes tops,' to be back out in the field, changed and ready to report to class after out daily doses of morning abuses--tough calisthenics and tougher runs in the Miami summer.

"They're fuckin with me too much man. Why me?--every time. I can't take it no more. I'm gonna fuckin explode."

"Hold on big fella. DeRose, listen--they see your size and they want to break you, but rise above it. You're a natural leader."

"I know. But damn. Enough is enough. Why?"

"They figure you can take anything. Keep your chin up. It'll pass. Soon you'll be on the force and you won't have to wait on the list like the rest of us."

I could see this was no consolation and realized by his expression as he shook his bald head tiredly that he'd figured out the trainers were tough on him for his connection. His uncle was friendly with one of the city's higher ups. I was his friend but hadn't probed.

"Let's go to class since our excessive abuse is over for today. You're a class favorite, remember? Not to mention class clown."

I got him there. His smile returned. DeRose wiped the last of his tears. I moved into the shower,

"See you out there," I said breathing a sigh of relief and reflected. He even looked intimidating while he was crying.

I felt like crying and quitting too. They had abused me harder than ever this morning; that's why I was late. They kept me and another white boy out doing pushups until our faces were ground into the mud. I scrubbed the caked dirt out now with what little effort I could, and with unfortunately no lather to assist me. But my debasing had not been cumulative. I was blessed with being able to follow commands easily and didn't screw up. DeRose, however, wasn't so blessed in that area. He was a bouncer at an exclusive club in South Beach. Many of the instructors on break had approached him about being let in for free. It was a little odd, them being in their early forties with wives and kids.

On the ride home, I placed the fire hat on top of the other gear, wary but prideful. I came to apply to the Fire Academy the spring after 9/11--ironically, not because of it as many others. I remember listening to Howard Stern on the way to a job fair up north when the first plane hit. It's ironic how comedy and tragedy are so often intermixed, as a ladder leaning on the building is supported by the rungs underneath it on the lower, smaller ladder which slides parallel on the same rescue mission.

Just the other day Lt. Gomez, with his limp, lectured with fire in his eyes how the tragedy of 9/11 had hit him for he had several NY firefighter friends in the midst of it.

He emphasized to us--"This job...be ready. And this goes to show--that tragedy in New York that anything and everything can happen. Never get complacent. If you think there's anything funny about this job," he glanced at DeRose, who put his head down shamefully for a moment, "you're wrong. Plain and simple. It's about being attentive, not just in the truck or at the fire, but everywhere. Maintaining your equipment, double and triple checking is the absolute minimum. Plain and simple. If you're scared about losing your life...this isn't the place for you. What are you going to do when a child is there and your captain sends you and your buddy in? You gonna go? Or not? It's a yes or no. Plain and simple. And if anyone is leaning towards anything than the affirmative answer, then there's the door. No thinking about that. Plain and simple. You be ready and you go. That's all I've got to say about that gentlemen. We're gonna go on a run. I knew George here told you my leg was bothering me too much to go. But I'm going. And if anyone loses to me, you better get ready for pushups cuz I ain't stopping. And no faking either, to any of you losers, I'll get every ounce of energy out of you come hell or high water. Plain and simple. Let's go.

The next morning DeRose and I were among the first recruits to arrive.

"Man, did you hear Lt. Tom in class talk about these TOPA inspections they do? Yo, I can't waits for dat…UMMM-UMMMPH."

"Theatre of Performing Arts," I responded. "It's funny how these firemen use anacronyms to instruct us and apparently even to brand their pleasure with interesting acrostics."

"Yo, call it what you want, but we get to inspect all the strip joints down here. What a perk," the younger man's hormones were raging before I could manage to slug my coffee down.

He continued, "Yo, I'd probably get major wood. Some one could light a match on my wanker and I'd go up in flames in that motherfucker. It'd be fresh yo."

"Uggh! I don't have the energy to think about sex--not with these early mornings week after week. It even fucks up my sleep schedule on the weekends being programmed to wake up."

"Shit. That's aight. Nothing compared to howz they gonna wake our asses up at the station, then slide down that pole."

"Uggh--into a truck equipped with blaring sirens. I'm having second thoughts."

"Come on man. We'ze almost through in this joint. Two more weeks."

"Hey. Is it really true you're hooked up with a job? Who is it? Maybe I can apply at the same station…"

"Shit--straighten up your desk. Gomez is about to jezet in'ear."

After Gomez's general berating, we pitched in for that day's snacks. I tried corralling DeRose, but we were being issued extra equipment for our run into the Firehouse. Practice with the gas mask would begin in the afternoon. As DeRose and I ate a Pan Con Bistec sandwich with our Cuban classmates, I expressed my anxiety.

"Listen. I want to stick close to you during practices. I'm no good with that regulator."

"Shit man, ain't you never been scuba diving down here--the Keys?"

"No. When I went I just snorkeled."

"Yeah sure. Don't worry. I'll help you out."

"Thanks."

The morning was beautiful. I was at the head of the run. I don't know how many laps ahead of Gomez. The air was crisp for a summer day, no humidity whatsoever. After I showered there was little soreness in my body given that it was Wednesday mid-week where I usually felt like the makings of a train wreck. I received my score for the prior day's test and was happy with it.

"Too bad about Jimmy," DeRose remarked.

"Such a nice kid," I agreed.

"Too nice. He's Haitian like me, but he's one that is too laid back for this job. Lackadaisical--I'm sure that's why Gomez ousted him."

"I heard the reason was that he failed the makeup quiz."

"That don't matter none. If they don't want you to graduate for one reason or another they'll get the slackers. We got nothing to worry about--me with enough demerits to spare in this last week and you, leading the pack most days on our run. The fire department needs guys like us to be an example held up for others.

The ex-chief now principal of the academy addressed us, "Gentlemen, you're into your final week and pending the last test…as you know the final test is a real fire drill in the Training house. You'll be one step closer to graduation and realizing your dreams of becoming firemen."

He was a distinguished man. Fifty-two who looked forty, with wisdom and great oratory skills. A steadiness one would expect in an accomplished leader. He not only held our attention with ease, but also got everyone quite fired up.

Afterward, I asked for a moment. We both stepped away from the dispersing group,

"I wanted to be sure," I began, "that this is the right career for me."

He replied, "I remember in your interview session, Mr. Strident, you told the class that your cousins in Boston on both sides of your family were on the department. Your Uncle Bud was a chief; her daughter recently became a firewoman. It's a job of pride, tradition. It gets in your blood. You know yourself. You'll make a fine fireman too. Now get ready for gas mask practice."

I managed a smile and immediately thought, on my walk back to the classroom, to obtain my gear, about the first story my dad used to read to me. On his lap in the living room couch with the orange rug and the yellow, white and tangerine fringed couch. He used to bounce my brother and me on his legs. The cover of the book was sky blue like the one I looked at today. The cover also showed a perky, hush puppyish basset hound with a red fire hat on and green hose walking past the ladder on the side of the red fire engine #2. I remember he looked excited in his work. Page after page, dedication was the theme, cleaning the station, checking the equipment, giving speeches to visitors on fire safety to young school children who'd come to learn of the honorable occupation. Then a dangerous fire broke out, a five-alarm fire. All the trucks went past his. The radio called for his unit to come quickly. He became nervous for the first time in the story as his puppy eyes gazed at the fires on the top floor of an apartment building, burning bright and threatening to reach the next building. And the story telling always ended with my dad saying, "but he had a job to do, and he did it! (with particular emphasis on the last four words).

I always laughed. My younger brother and I requested the story often and then gleefully repeated the last line aloud with dad until bedtime was postponed numerous times.

The next day I spoke with Katherine. She asked me if I was okay.

"No. I'm exhausted. I' working nights and I can't get any sleep. Everything's fuzzy. I've gotta be honest--I don't think I'm ever going to get the hang of that regulator. After we practiced yesterday, I was just as lost. And I'm getting the order of things messed up. I'm not mechanical enough for this job. I'm tired…"

"I'm tired too. I work six days a week and part of me wants to quit too. But you just gotta push through it. Tell you what--if I'm in your group, I'll show you how to do it."

I looked at her slight blond frame and marveled at her toughness, an inner strength. She'd struggled at times on the physicalness of the academy training but the mental capacity…she was miles ahead of me.

"Thanks," I said, grateful no one overheard our private conversation.

This afternoon was tougher. The Spanish steak was repeating on me as we did calisthenics. The principal, Mike Kiels was watching, taking in the morning and seemed slightly more amused for there was an instructor taking over the first half of the morning drills. He was even tougher than Gomez. He'd have to be to scare DeRose like he did. I recalled the first day when DeRose and I watched in terror as this Sergeant Diptoly met us in a downpour in the middle of one of our runs. He drove into the middle of the group, screeching tires and hopped out before the car even came to a halt, bolting from the red vehicle like water pressure emitted from a built up pressure hose ready to explode--and he did, prompting DeRose to say at that day's lunch. That crazy Diptoley…I'm really not afraid of anyone, my whole life…But he scares the hell out of me, yo!

Diptoly summarized our ineptness on the morning run, "Too many people were slacking so we're gonna stay out here in this heat at least an extra half hour for every violation I find. First one:

"DeRose. Your belt is off. Strident. Yours too. Drop down and give me twenty."

"Slewstein--why you looking at DeRose? Your eyes should be straight ahead."

"According to my tally that's an hour and half in this SWELTERING HEAT!"

"We're going to run the obstacle course first though--and the last two to finish in each group of five...fifty push ups."

As I did my fifty, I could see DeRose looking sympathetically at me to finish up. But Diptoly didn't see DeRose; his eyes were still on me.

"Why you looking at DeRose? Eyes straight ahead during pushups and keep your head up higher. Your visor is hitting the ground. You look discombobulated. I ain't gonna graduate anyone who is discombobulated and not ready for this job--too many other individuals down here are vying for your oppositions."

I heard a new voice interrupt loudly.

"That's right. Plain and simple keep your head up and not only that but you're supposed to be shouting out the number you're on...and loudly. Now as a group we're going to do six inches. Don't let your cap fall off. Lift your head off the ground enough so it doesn't scrape the ground."

As Gomez counted our third set, I swore that the nerves in my shoulder would give out. I'd aggravated an old Giu-jitsu injury by dragging the big sand dummy a few weeks ago with one hand to show how macho I was, and to impress a sexy blond recruit with legs up too her shoulders. I fantasized about bending her over a hydrant, wet n' wild with hoses draped around her naked blond tanned shoulder. I thought of something DeRose said about being on the firemen calendar--being ogled by women that he'd brag he was a fireman, of being a hero, and rescuing little children.

What were my dreams? Were they like that? Just because my cousins were firemen and woman, did I really have it in my blood? I'd never fantasized about rescuing a little child. Should I have? Did Mike Kiel really believe I'd be a good fireman?

I asked him that again after practice as we walked by the fence near the highway by his office.

"You had trouble securing your hat out

there I see," he smiled.

"I still haven't learned the regulator and we've got that drill coming up on Saturday with the real fire, not to mention I can't identify or use the many tools the job requires.

"The mechanical part of the job can be learned...pretty much by anybody."

He continued, "I will tell you that if you want the closeness of good people on the job looking out for each other--it's right here. It's the best place in the workplace for cohesion...real cohesion amongst coworkers. You won't find it in the corporate world, or any place else. Firemen are the best breed period."

"I know. And I really like that. But I just feel other people could do a better job than I could."

"Well," he sighed, "it's up to you. Only you know. But give it some more thought. Or maybe become an inspector. There are all types of jobs in the department besides being a firefighter."

"I think I have given it enough thought already chief. I wish you and the rest of the recruits and instructors all the best."

"Likewise."

171

DeRose called me up, "Man, I can't believe it's true. I talked to the chief yesterday and with only two days to go you left. Why?"

"I don't know. I just didn't have what it takes. My dreams are taking me elsewhere. I've busy writing my book. You save lives and be careful at the TOPA inspections."

Truth was I read an article about pornos being watched and how they may've influenced a fireman to harass a female employee. I didn't want to be part of such a family--not matter how cohesive.

Regardless of the results of my decision, regret it not. Living up to the fairy tale dreams of possibly becoming a hero of having a job to do and he did it,' the basset hound chant which haunted me on a daily basis as all my other bullshit jobs in South Florida. I should have stuck it out like Katherine and DeRose.

One day, however, an article made me glad that I did quit.

In 2003 in Port Everglades, a fire recruit, named Wayne Mitchell lost his life when pursing said dream of becoming a firefighter. The recruits were to enter a ship with two fires simultaneously going on; no safety officers, supervisors, or ambulance standing by. No walk through beforehand for the untested in real live fire recruits. No rapid intervention teams of firefighters to rush the building-ship in case of an emergency. Poor Wayne Mitchell, eerily my age got separated during the fire from his two classmates and several officers just like I did on my crawl through in the darkness during a maze exercise in a practice tower. I remember sweating and no supervisor or instructor was present. I finally ripped off the mask as I was gasping for air.

Suddenly the instructor appeared, "You can't do that," the TOPA story instructor reprimanded. "You did a good job though," he commended my classmate who was linked to me; so I failed to see the mazy evaluation between poor job and good job.

As I write this I'm reading the county's report dated November 4th, but really just last Tuesday.

'The Battalion Chief (of the Departments Fire-Rescue Union), said the report, "raises several serous concerns but disturbingly unqualified supervisors were called in who didn't have the proper training and to boot no one inside the building was carrying a radio. Inside, the building was so hot that two of the instructors bailed out through the emergency exits, leaving only one instructor to guide the recruits out. No one realized Mitchell was missing until his exhausted classmates stumbled out of the building; they were all suffering from burns or heat street,' the report said.

I discussed the article with DeRose, who was due to report to work for his first day of duty on the department, the day after tomorrow.

"Yeah, but the training sequence was all out of order--That group of guys weren't even taught search and rescue before that live fire exercise. The whole course curriculum was out of sequence."

"Be careful. And be ready," I cautioned him.

DeRose answered, "Plain and simple."

THE END

8 - Road Trip

We all love a wild time. And this trip promised to be, no not simply promise, rather a guarantee, of a wile spree. I brought plenty of bail money--seriously. Me and my buddy Rick have spent a night or two in the clink though never together. I'm Brent from Connecticut. Well, neither one of us were hardened criminals and not even given over to deceitfulness toward others in the common way. No, not at all. We were gentlemen.

The most fun I ever had was the summer we worked together. Elephant malt liquor, pitchers at lunch, nips at night breaks. It never ended. Luckily, the manager didn't find out about our shenanigans until it was too late. In late August Rick went back to California to model ski-wear and I returned to college for my final year.

After graduation despite taking two spring breaks in consecutive months with different hard charging crews from separate reckless partying schools, mere months for a fresh plan of itinerant inclination, I tossed my tasseled cap in the air and instead succumbing as classmates may, to mailing resumes cross country, I expressly delivered myself to Rick's mother-in-law's ranch house in Reno for a spring skiing expedition.

Rick said weather permitting we may be in for an eyeful of 'hot snow bunnies' in nowhere near winter gear, flailing flesh while spreading fresh tracks with long limbs sprouting above pink boots glistening and sliding along, bouncingly tracing soft, deep tracks of lumpy powder fine snow, as Easter Bunnies on stylish skis delivering treats.

Upon picking me up, Rick began laying out our itinerary. Couple days in Reno, then off to Santa Clara to see some relatives, then to San Francisco to visit an ex-girlfriend, next to San Jose to see an old friend of his and back to Reno to chill for a day or two.

He was dressed preppily as if he went to Stanford. I knew he had partied there with some of his wild, well known ski buds, but he'd been thrown off the Colorado ski team in his second season for wild behavior, not just a problem drinker like me but LSD, angel dust, mushrooms and many other pills were in the mix. But he assured me that he'd cut way down on the hard stuff, 'now just booze and juana, dude,' I recalled him telling me on the way back into the phone company building for whom we worked; this particular night we almost got fired on our last scheduled shift together. I'd dropped the disk/tapes all over the floor. Rick came to my defense and the female supervisor smelled our breaths,

"You guys go out every break and get…get…lit up like a Christmas tree.'

We thought that was the funniest thing we ever heard.

Leslie with the grey eyes and tight beige wool-knit sweater with round large breasts shouting 'look at me' asked me about what happened after the supervisor in a librarian, squealy pitched voiced harkened the manager. Leslie, clearly down because she'd been unable to reach Rick who was flying back to California, was interested in the last morsel of information she could pilfer from me, his closest bud.

"Oh," I explained, "he just cussed us out and said he should've fired us weeks ago but for me to finish up today. I' heading to school anyhow. What about you and Rick? Are you still going to go out with him?"

"No. We spent a few weeks together, but I have a serious boyfriend. He was away. So...it's not right--but it happened," she said without hinting toward shame, but too down to be harder on herself than the situation perhaps warranted.

I understood. Rick possessed the type of power, magnetism regarding women or people in general.

And I felt uncomfortable under this spell now as his green eyes cast a wide sense of purposeful threat into the air and picked up my trepidation, pulling as if a fish finder's transducer emitting its warning waves from the bottom pulling up in a wide funnel-scope any palpitations of organisms struggling in the chain of survival to disperse from detection of the anglers perched above with technologies to sweep into a perilous view. The eyes bore into me as I grabbed my fork then pretended to squint at the smoke, but he locked on my wide-eyed spheres. I covered my general nervousness by scraping the salt off my margarita and licked it. He continued to scrutinize everything while fixing more intensely on my pupils, which must have been shaking. He'd been asking me about my school year and I searched for an interesting story while trying to maintain his gaze, the wild eyes, like an animal, a rabid hungry panther. What was he showing his domination over me for? There weren't even any chicks at our table. Maybe he was looking at a table behind us. I'd have to look; but I didn't want to give into the cat and mouse stare-down. So I ratcheted up my intensity, shining my brown eyes seriously back into him while dropping my voice. He leaned back in his chair and craned his head a bit to consider my deeper bass voice, but the eyes though, a further distance back what I thought would be less intimidating in a retreat, were still locked on me, unsympathetic, cold callous. It belied his good natured, super-friendly, killer-dude, persona, but also made me hardly any less skeptical in the respect that bringing bail money was a smart investment. I was always the rowdiest in my school, kicked off campus, the biggest drinker in the drunkest house on campus.

But I was a poser next to Rick; my eyes twitching in a strabismus unequal to his binocular clasping green fire eyes, which derisively crumbled my brown set. I lost track of my conversation, the pace of my voice faltered. As I cut into my chicken fajita, I meekly cleared my throat to distract the fact that the panther had melted down the mouse across from him. Now we could get on with the week-long adventure.

"I hope you don't mind, or uh, I just want to thank you for letting me come along. I mean, I know it's your only week of this whole year."

"No problem Brent. You are going to love the west coast and the ladies too."

That comment right there was enough to intimidate me. But as it turned out at Squaw Valley, I didn't have anything to worry about for we didn't hang out at the lodge or even the apres-ski nightlife. But I knew the dreaded moment would come when Rick would score and I'd scramble to do the same. It meant I would need more liquid courage. Well, no problem there. With Rick there was never a chance of going dry, no matter what the circumstances. He was a bloodhound, not to be denied, a predator of a different order--a panther.

I rolled off the waterbed as Rick came out

of the shower.

"Let's go dude. We are heading to Frisco. It's quite a drive."

"I know. You have any eggs we can fry up? Toast?"

"No man. We'll stop for some donuts when we gas up if you need some fuel."

If...I thought. How could Rick survive a long drive on only a few donuts? It sounded as if the concept of breakfast was alien. I knew I couldn't survive this part of the road trip on a liquid only diet. Maybe that's how he stays so thin. I appeared healthy and fit, like a coach, with my white sweatshirt, the air of responsibility; and he looked preppy yet dangerous--a combination which women rendered incapable of resisting.

Speaking of danger, as we headed to San Fran (via Sacramento), I felt a panoply of emotion as we headed up airborne on a double black diamond at Squaw. On the chairlift, beside Rick, I turned behind us to see and agree to the observation that the view was mighty impressive--the white snow herded and heaped as a fully thick down sleeping bag, groomed immaculately, waiting to melt but the temperature never dipped so we saw no bikinis on the slope but in the crisp air as we climbed steeper to the summit, I saw in Rick's black polarized sunglasses our image, our scarved faces wrapped suavely, tanned bearing our natural sheen, fashioning us as models in a postcard, pasted against the pristine backdrop of Lake Tahoe, a pool of an immense blue pupil emerging from the snowy wonderland-scape, surrounding the deep mysterious glass loch. No clouds were between us on the lift, and the serene wild third eye of nature below, spying us climbing Squaw, no flaws in the stunning vistaview.

But now I peered under the lift's crossbar holding us in, directly under the left foot, past my one size too tiny ski boots, and two sizes too large racing skis, both borrowed from Rick for my first packed deep powder western ski experience. Rick had instructed me in the difference between west coast skiing as opposed to east coast; but the petrifying moguls the size of small stores, dotted and ingrained terrain below. And I saw piked rocks emerging from select and yet seemingly more evident patches upon closer examination with plenty of trees on the outskirts to worry about cracking my head or other bodily part on. About a score of feet that would be traced in the warring air by my tingling cramped ski boot warning me before alighting on the deep powder…Shit I didn't know if I could deposit myself on the slope from that moment of suspension from chair to air to mountain without falling into other sophisticated west coast skiers. I saw how steep it was even from up here and oh shit some of the skiers were nearly bumping into each other. I'd definitely get mine crossed with some one, I was sure. I made up my mind.

"Rick--I can't do this."

"What are you talking about? You will be fine. Relax."

"No. I'm serious. I'm not getting off. I'm going to ride the chair back down."

He struggled to suppress a laugh as a smile began to break but he quickly cut it short and pursed his lips coolly.

"You are going to be able to do it. You want to be able to tell everyone dude that you skied a double black diamond…at Squaw no less!"

This normally would have appealed to my ego. And it'd be great to impress chicks with too on the remainder of this road trip. How fearless in the face of uncharted territory I was and dangerous and brave, against all odds wasn't it? As I was on racing skis too large, boots too tight, and skiing on packed west coast powder for the first time. A virgin who broke his cherry on a sharp, piercing rock hard double diamond. Temptingly to a mountebank. But I was already routed in my decision as I'd ever been anyway stoutly as these moguls were packed against the mountains. Unmovable. I would sit and not care if my butt became part of the snow tram as icicles attached on the superfluously, majestic and even more ominous Palisades trail, the cliffs climbing nearby but a good distance off from us; of which Rick slipped in the fact he jumped a mere 75 feet off the cliff last year rendering my attempt minute compared to that stuff of manhood of Everest proportion. God was that beautiful; the Palisade a Mount Rushmore without the pols. I laid my poles across my lap and said,

"I'll wait for you at the lodge."

Rick removed his glasses and with green panther eyes lifted the arm of the chair and said,

"Pick up those poles off your lap and get ready. You are going." He turned his head away. I gulped. "Just follow me," he added,

"I won't let you fall."

I believed him…foolishly. Though I didn't bang into anyone upon debarking, I did proceed to fall halfway down the face of the mountain. Rick was a sport waiting for me. I didn't know how he could see me. It seemed like he was always a quarter mile ahead of me with moguls possessing verticality of pine trees, interrupting our field of vision; or maybe that was the snow caked into my foggy goggles. I did feel great about having conquered the double diamond. Maybe I had hope after all. Rick's magical confidence had already rubbed off on me. I hoped the chicks from here on out could sense this aura.

San Francisco Slide Show

We entered the bar on a rainy San Fran night to see Jake Jo Mama at a comedy club. Rick's ex introduced me to her friend, a blind date for me. She was nice but too heavy. I didn't even bother to check out her face. I listened intently to the comedian and patiently awaited the night to close; when it concluded on an uncomfortable couch just outside our shoulder haired blond host's bedroom where Rick was making his moves. Taking some solace in her stalwart stance against his pressing advances, whereby she purported her allegiance to her boyfriend. I would hear her pleadings clearly,

"I've been going out with him for four years. I told you over the phone...there's no way. You should be sleeping out there with your friend."

Rick answered her, "Where? There is no room. That floor is so hard Gail," he stroked her thread-like corporate hair coaxing the moxie chick to loosen her prissiness.

"Don't touch. I'll send you out there still...I mean it!"

"All right. I just think--we're perfect together. We both like to ski. Are you sure you can't call in tomorrow? We came all this way. And Brent wants to show off. Bring Angela again."

"He doesn't even like her," she illustrated with an eyebrow shot toward the window shades.

"They just met. Give it time," he deflected.

"I don't think they're a match. Even if they were, I'm way too busy at work."

187

On and on it went. My eyes drifted off in uncertainty as to Rick's score.

Nothing awoke me but I knew the outcome from their glows as I ate my muffin alone, while they finished their showers and got ready to tackle the day.

"Rick pass me a beer," I said annoyed.

He opened the fridge and flipped on with a smile. We left dropping her off in the financial district.

I wanted to keep my buzz going so Rick pulled into a package store after heading down crooked Lombard Street, we scurggled Sapporo, a Japanese beer and I fantasized about geishas. We'd tour Telegraph Hill and Pier 39 before pointing ourselves to Santa Clara to see his Uncle.

When we arrived he was fixing something in the shower. Rick couldn't control his laughter as Renny swore nonstop. He was a former tight end for the Niners, gangly. You guys want to watch some porn?"

"Sure. But won't your old lady be home soon?" I inquired.

"She'll be cooking dinner," the gangly formation of a man mumbled.

I flicked my eyes across the close proximity of the kitchen and the lounge area where we were. And when Renny's eyes hit upon mine, I shrugged with a look that said, 'There are no doors.' Then with palms open as if to say, 'You do realize that sound travels, don't you?'

Renny piped up, "I'm always watching them so...don't bother her none. Then to Rick, "Shit. Drive me over to the hardware store Rick. We're outta fucking the right screws--and fuck me."

Rick grabbed his suede brown leather coat and flung it briskly over his shoulder, reached into his pockets and jingled his keys. His smile was almost as unguarded as a child's now and held in a giggle which despite his concerted efforts escaped. He winked at me as if Renny was the single funniest human being this side of the Mississippi.

As the door shut, and I stayed behind, all I knew was that I was hungry and his wife had a chicken to cook and it'd be awhile before dinnertime. The other thought was-- Wow. Look at those tapes. I bet their all porn. This could fill the idle time. But it wouldn't be a wise decision to have his wife who I'd never met, confront a stranger in her quaint Santa Clara abode watching the Simi Valley's best cavort on her living room screen. What if I wanted to rub one out? This black leather would show if I wasn't careful to catch myself with tissues. Where wee the tissues? I looked curiously, went into the kitchen to check a few cabinets and still couldn't find anything. Naw. It wasn't worth the risk.

Ten minutes later I heard a car. It was her. She said hi and excused herself for dinner preparations. Such a sweet girl. At dinner, it became apparent that they had a loose marriage bond, but the passion appeared to be out of the picture and I knew it wasn't due to the cook, but Renny's rancid tape collection. I wondered how long they'd been married or when their sex life embered out.

On the drive out, Rick illuminated how cool Jane his wife was, 'she's into those pornos too.'

I wondered if Rick ever made a move on her. I didn't know if he respected the institution of marriage. It wasn't something I felt I could ask him no matter how drunk we were. He filled me in on his own escapades that would've topped any of Renny's VCR tapes. Secretly, I wanted one of those highlights to be part of our road trip reel--

'could be me or him I don't care.'

I let him in on that much. We clinked drinks and sped off into the night air of Carmel where we stopped at the Hog's Breath Inn. But strangely, there were no broads, single anyhow, and no Clint; on Pebble Beach Golf Course, we did spot a woman walking outside from the lodge's parking lot, a woman who resembled Sandra Locke. We took pictures outside the aquarium where seals played in the cool surf. It was good clean fun. One bright uncompetitive moment among buds on a road trip where ultimately the unspoken tally was number of beers drained and number of girls filled. It was a relief to head into the car with tunes and booze, movements finally with illicit road trip tales of old told to pass the time until the next cities' opening line strophe. But before opening the car door we had admitted we did feel a little gay about posing stationary together for so many shots.

San Jose Shots

All I did was shots for 'pregaming' which continued unabated until arriving at the ultra cool beach theme wide assorted club separated by two very large glass double doors, Club Spun. However, well before departing for the club and in fact at the beginning of our imbibing, Rick's old friend had welcomed us into his home and showed us the layout where we'd 'sleep.'

Rick smugly said, "Yeah, but we won't be sleeping alone."

"Certainly, I won't," he added in a sagacious bid to smear my chances.

Something in me felt challenged. I shot him a look like Rocky gave Apollo Creed when his pride was hurt. Jason noticed this and saw my face; he felt compelled to say,"

"You know...you two look like brothers, or cousins--something."

I beamed and Rick took it as an insult.

"I don't think so. Have another beer," he said in the dark room downstairs.

"Yeah, I need one," I said and led the charge upstairs to the pure white mecca fridge filled with Sierra Nevada Pale Ale. After mixing the bready malt with sugary worms of tequila shot with the end result twirling in our tongues the slow stickiness with left the roofs of our mouths wanting not to savor but to crave more...more.

At Club Spun, I felt uncomfortable by the pool. It was too well lit. The women were dressed too preppy for my preference. I stayed with the slutty-glammed out gals in the club's dance floor area. I hated disco so. I kept doing tequila shots and when I lost track of Rick, who was hooking up with a short sexy Latin brunette, my scurries became more frequent between rooms branding me as a loser with each subsequent dash of inadequacy in gradations --each mad dash more meaningless hence degrading than the last.

I don't remember how we got home only that Jason seemed to think I took no shit from any bouncers,' as he assisted me to my bed on this leg of the trip. Amid the spin, I wondered where Rick was. He finally came in turning on the lamp on the oak table.

I asked, "What happened to the brunette?"

"She was fun but I got Cathy here," a bloodshot blond walked into the room and didn't seem to mind Rick's openness about his fun comment with a floosie; Rick acknowledged the freeness with a knowing wink. This one wanted a thrashing at the panther's paws. Rick grabbed something small from his drawer and jammed it in his pants pocket and took the girls arm in a sweeping jerking motion that had them careening down the hall. I heard the garage and pondered why he bothered going out again at all, for what he had to make short work of didn't require the outdoors. Inside I slept restlessly alone and the fucking heater wouldn't come back on. How could California be so cold?

Post Cards

It was a relief to return to Reno as we passed the Bonanza Ranch with light snowflakes flaking as moths lazily lilting round a light though it was a gray gloomy day. Rick braked to his mailbox and bounced out seemingly as a kid about to empty his stocking on Christmas morning. He held what looked like thirty or more post cards with an unsurprised manner. He rifled through them quickly. Halfway through--

"Yes!" he separated this one from the pack for some reason with extreme gusto.

"What?" I asked as he tossed the rest haphazardly strewn across the backseat. One had landed in my lap. It was signed Debbie after a long bodied salutation given over to many exclamations.

"She's in town," Rick shook his head in negative disbelief but with a smiled that betrayed his shaking head, issued as if waiting for a messiah. How could he have lost faith? Now laughing.

"Who?"

"This Japanese girl--Francine. She wants to go out tonight."

"Looks like you're bound to score again!" I tried to inject some enthusiasm for Rick's roll--soon to be sushi take out--on the go!

"Don't worry. It says here she's got a friend. This chick is doing a pilot as he read a bit more of the postcard.

"Which one?"

"Francine."

"What is the other girls name?"

"She doesn't mention it."

"Oh."

We dressed and I loaded up on cologne just in case. Rick looked as good as I've ever seen him.

"Man, we're going to get ripped tonight. I just spoke to my friend Matt and he's treating us to dinner for a Saint Paddie's Day party."

"But this is May."

"To Matt--he's Irish--he parties hard every month on the seventeenth regardless of the season's time."

I didn't know if I could keep up. But I would valiantly try. I was no wuss. No, I could chug and I would score. I gelled my hair again, spiking it just right. I looked at the waterbed. Firm up pal we're doing some pushing later on.

Halfway through the goblets of green beer, God knows how Matt arranged this; the brown curly head visible above the crowded bar weaved in and out expertly in his athletic build. His irresistible full, rosy cheeks glowing pink contrasted with soft blue protuberant excited shiny eyes must have endeared the thirsty crowd to part as yet again Matt would come around with either beer or shots faster than we could down them, even during the large dinner. I felt gorged.

"What time are we supposed to meet the girls?"

No one even heard me. We left the restaurant at some point.

Next thing I remember is Matt walking abreast of us pointing out the best bars in the casino, where we should commence our Scorpion Bowl race. What the hell is he doing here? I thought so I asked Rick who responded,

"The girls won't mind if he shows up."

"But does he have a seat at the table? I assume he needs a ticket to the show."

"He'll pull up a chair if there's not enough room. Are you excited to see ShaNaNa?"

"I guess," I answered.

"What about Chantelle?" he arched his eyebrows as if I should be ecstatic to see what? essentially a 50's group?

"Performing," he added.

"Who? Doing what?"

"Chantelle--the girl from last night that you were dancing with."

I vaguely remembered talking about some show with the girl at some point that evening.

I answered, "Well, I know she'll be here but what's she doing, performing during intermission some type of sing-song, theatrical tableside something or other?"

"No dude. She's part of the group," he laughed.

My mouth froze open.

"She's the one who gave us front row tickets and free drinks."

The free drinks were screwdrivers. We had two complimentary drinks each and somehow Matt got so loud that it almost caused the performers to stop playing.

After the show I was so blitzed I couldn't even stand up and I was leaning with one hand against a large marble column just at the entrance of the concert room with slots about ten feet behind my head which Chantelle gazed at when there was a lull in my conversation.

"Sooo--yull callll uh me when jew get at…er too…Boston," I slurred.

Chantelle answered, "We're taping the show then flying out."

The Japanese girl who'd been eavesdropping pulled away from Rick's tight grip surprisingly lightning quick that Rick teetered from side to side with a look that said he expected that embrace to end in such a fashion.

From under Francine's dark wispy bangs and sultry duskiness in her burgundy skimpy halter dress, which matched her equally full upper and lower lips chimed in,

"Speaking of flight, we have the red-eye."

Chantelle said, "Yes we really must be going," with an oh-so sorry smile. She was sincere. I didn't want to sound desperate so I didn't pine. I wanted to leave her with my cavalier attitude that I displayed at the Limelight Club the prior night where we danced.

She had approached me..."Want to dance?" her white skirt flowed out from tanned track legs, not tall but gams that cointantly (Curly of Three Stooges) knocked at your groin.

"No," I answered and watched her bristle before I broke into a wide flirtatious smile and enveloped her wrist with a tight tug that spilled us onto a dance floor where we twisted then grinded and slow danced for the night.

Outside the casino as Rick and I walked aimlessly before locating our car, I explained the ultra cool delivery of that line and I included her rapturous smell that tickled my olfactory inlet. I further explained that last night was the night I could've and should've scored with Chantelle if her Japanese friend hadn't have had to audition for that pilot so damn early.

I continued, "And aren't you bummed

that you couldn't nail Francine?"

This seemed to trigger something. I could see that he was now enlightened to the effect of going pussyless on back to back nights; and with some one he'd wanted to bed as badly as anyone in that large stack of feline postcards. I wondered how long it had been since he last checked the mailbox. Was that a season's worth piled up? A month's worth? Or a week's worth? He used his mother-in-law's sparingly but I was under the impression he'd been mostly held down at the ranch house of late, though he was traveling on minor road trips to see buds and the scores of his chicks. It would be uncool to ask, I delimited my curiosity as we peeled out with more force than ever in his Supra.

"Hey Rick--slow down."

"I want to make good time."

"Why?"

"I'm hungry."

This was a first.

"At three in the morning? We ate like kings not too long ago."

"I don't know if there are any restaurants around here. That's why I'm speeding. I want to cook breakfast as soon as we get home."

"Do you? Shit Rick!!"

He took the exit overpass as if he were a cop chasing a fugitive.

"Trying to get us killed?" I asked terrified.

Rick stared straight ahead with an overbite so solemn and gripped the steering wheel tighter. I scrambled to think of something to say to calm his rising temper.

"Do you realize your swerving?"

"I'm driving fine," his pupils bulged sideways to slap my criticism back in the passenger side where he wanted my back seat driving to stay. He explained for my benefit, "I always drive better drunk."

That's my line I thought. But it certainly wasn't true here I easily deduced even in my own stupor.

After more time passed, I said, "Let me drive. I feel great--you are all over the road."

"Fuck no man. I'm in control. I'll get us home. Besides, my buzz is less than when we first started driving."

I waited and kept thinking maybe his weaving would lessen; but after having gripped the wheel twice to steady the Supra, he still said,

"Not much longer."

An hour went by, "Rick, we're going in

the wrong direction."

Steam came out his ears transmitting anger toward me. And his green eyes with hazel around the edges were set in a water pool of mixed red thin capillaries veining into the white hawkish shape of his eyes which made the water part uncool, distorting the hawk set definition around them.

I felt the car slow. His grip loosened on the wheel as he pulled slowly into the breakdown lane. He shifted into park and said, "Even with the distance, you on the east and me on the west coast...we never see each other and rarely ever talk on the phone...But..." his voice quaked, "You're my best friend," he sobbed a hundred sobs as I put my arm around his suede covered shoulders.

That moment of clarity saved our lives that night. It was, I surmised, one of many times subsequently for Rick and myself, and countless other imbibers on wild road trips that such moments came.

As I enter into my third year of recovery and my ninth step, I wonder if Rick's star had become brighter. I'm quite sure-- if God got him out of bars.

Epilogue

He ducked and craned his head unable to pry his gaze away from viewing the moon through the driver-side glass of the most recent dings and dents his Supra undertook.

The highly polished gold coin rose through the white clouds, which were a diagonal vent as the orb slid through a series of slotted abbreviated cirrus strip vapors in the Orange County night; the whole scene only a slight around sliver, encompassed in an indigo circular frame; this aforementioned torn portion of lighter discoloration, immediately locking the nightscape, barely distinct from the bigger picture of the abnormally bright night because it was so beautiful…so different.

The traffic began to move and he reluctantly took his foot off the brake and gave gas to slowly roll past the stoplight. No one beeped at him but even if they did he would continue to keep his neck craned at that forty-five degree angle instead of on the nine o'clock traffic ahead. He ruminated on the difference between beautiful and different. Did one cause the other? His interpretation was if something's different, that is precisely what makes it beautiful. Yes. He knew that's what he thought. Why didn't he reverse the order when he inherently placed beautiful first? How many others shared his inclination?

He suddenly noticed a star as he pulled out of the bar. From the moment he put the key in his ignition, he pondered the meaning of it as he exited the bar alone. Rick didn't want to open the mailbox the next morning. Someone at the bar had given him a number of a program that he planned on calling.

THE END

9 - S FL Telemarketers

The sharp young man, a Mexican stomped on the cig and exhaled the last drag. Shaking his head, down, for a change, he deadpanned to me,

"What did I do in another life to deserve this?"

He was sad but he broke into a wide convincing grin so quickly that it made me forget instantaneously the hurt he'd been displaying, evidently for a prolonged period.

This Mexican trained me one day when I was selected to move from the training Basic Room to the more advanced Pre-1003, the larger division of selling mortgages and home equity lines; those in Pre1003 were distinguished because they received commissions. But those in Pre10 were still on the front-line, making phone calls and getting a 'lead' for the loan officer to close it later, who collected proportionately much higher commissions than Pre10.

I noticed Ray making a line next to a Wells Fargo campaign, a company for which we called on the Basic side too, albeit the scope of requirements would become much narrower in Pre10. He had several leads on prior days as I viewed his daily recordings of them, but only one today. Ray seemed a bit tenser as a few half hours passed along. I wasn't too impressed with his pitch, but he was at the top of the board I realized; one very important thing from Ray I observed was his friendly phone manner:

"Oh...How you doing?" he'd say to the client like Joey on Friends; that everyday man style worked for him rather than knowledge, content, or substance in any form. We looked similar and sounded the same too. I decided right then and there that my approach here would be not to pressure, or impress, or dazzle, but simply put my arm around the customer like Old Abe Lincoln used to profess, 'If you would win a man to your cause, become his sincere friend first.'

He now addressed me, while scanning the stats on the big board of the other telephone reps between a lapse in calls during our training session, "Damn, that girl caught up. She was way behind on Tuesday, then the last couple days she came out of nowhere to pass me.

"What do you get if you're on top of the board?" I asked.

"Oh--every week we have a top producer so you get a $25.00 gift certificate to Publix Groceries. I've won it recently. So my baby can eat good lately." He smiled at the picture on his desk of his three year old child on the beach.

Since that day, it had been awhile that Ray and I had spoke to each other until Ray asked on break,

"Don't worry. It'll pick up for you. How many leads you have? I hear you've been doing great since you came over with us."

"I've got five so far."

"See--that's good."

"I gotta do something else...besides this phone work," he lamented.

"I've been thinking about writing a book."

"I wrote one."

"Yeah! What? Fiction or nonfiction?"

"Fiction."

"Wow, that's good. I want to do one on my life. I escaped from a Mexican prison. And…shit. I don't know why I'm telling you this--could you help me out?"

"I don't ghost write. Sorry. It sounds interesting. So just go ahead and write it. I think you can find one on-line. I'll be happy to read some of your first draft if you need any help or after you finish see me. I've made some connections, not only in publishing but also people in the movie biz--big stars."

"Let's get back on the phone" Ray said.

Big Scott rolled trough the crowd milling outside in the heat by the parking lot.

"Break's over. Get inside!"

As we walked to our seats, Ray exclaimed, "I'd like to read a copy of your book."

"Okay--when it comes out."

"When?"

"I think…next month."

Months flew by. My book wasn't out. I'd

made corrections. It was backed up; then the endorsements, three of them cam through but I was waiting for one last big one before going to print.

I took the telemarketing job, my fourth one in three years. I only took it because it seemed different. Most prominently among my observations, were the telemarketers' cubicles; the inside walls of virtually each block adorned with passages from the Bible. This must be a company that cares. And care was in evidence in the weekly Rewards meeting on Friday before our weekly mid-afternoon pizza party. No matter who won the award, the applause was deafening and not simply a short burst either, but a prolonged, heartfelt, rejoicing and regaling of that weeks' recipients accomplishment; a regaling fit for a king I fashioned. And they were sincere. How did they con the customers? Or were they really helping them with the noncommittal company's services?

I must have felt the latter for I believed it was honorable, assisting people in the purchase of their dream homes, or alleviating their debits, or providing cash to pay for hospital bills, or with an unsecured loan, perhaps to repair a dilapidated roof.

But would my job be secure. We all had to produce, and under dire circumstances. For Lionel would light the fire every Wednesday nonstop from 12:30 to 3:30. He was the supervisor. Charles Barkley in stature and in mouth, especially mouth. He gave everyone a headache. His scream of updates would pervade the building.

"Who's bringing one in?!…Venus Williams. Burt Sussman--Get off the phone and to the next one."

And to the whole room,, "Don't bother filling in the screens when you're through with the lead. As soon as the customer is gone, I want you gone too, and on to the next call."

Of course, that would piss off Quality Control; they wanted all the information on the application accurate for a smooth perusal once the application made its way to the loan officers' desk. A constant tug-of-war and many fire and brimstone meetings fueling Lionel's ire for that day's shift.

"Whose got one? We need it. We need to pay the light bill!"

Was he serious? No one knew. He kept the telephone reps in the dark, there and everywhere. 'Spiffs (incentives) for the next lead get to leave fifteen minutes early,' he'd promise.

"Yeah right. The list must be lost. No one leaves early," Venus apprised me. "These fools promise everything. They play you."

"Great and how am I supposed to pay my mortgage?" I asked.

"Work as much overtime now as you can cuz you never now. Especially you, with your high SPH (sales per hour). They want you people to work Saturdays and stay late during the night cuz you're producing. But me, I've got to change my pitch. I'm not happy with it no more. It's too monotone. What you say Burt? You be smooth-talking them. Don't you?"

"I don't know." But I knew the real reason was that I'd made a concerted effort to walk closer with Jesus and live in the spirit. I'd declined invitations to party with Playboy Playmates in South Beach, which I alluded to Ray once concerning my movie star connections. And as I saw it my high SPH was how the Lord rewarded me--top producer and three bonus checks in a row.

I didn't tell her that--though I should have. Instead, I said, "I just think of how many I want t do before I come in. That way I know where I'm going and I usually get there."

"Hmm. I do that too. But actually a lot of people here do too. Don't you see? They write the number five or six on their desk to remind them that that's what there s'post to get on their shift."

"But that's unrealistic. It's just wall paper after awhile, I imagine; it wears off."

"Ha! You crazy Burt. Maybe you right though. I just knowze I gots to switch my lame-ass pitch."

"Tell them you'll get them Anna Kournikova's autograph."

"Ha! That's true. Some of them, they be telling me, 'You played well at Wimbledon.'"

"But Burt--you must be telling them they won the lottery or some shit. I don't know. Okay, drop me off here. I'm gonna get the bus. You don't know how much I appreciate it. Just turn around and there's your street. You don't wanna get lost down here in Da Hood."

"See you tomorrow," I glanced at her strong jawline.

"Bye Burt." Venus withdrew her hand from the ashtray and then walked across the street like a black Elvira past her prime, arched barely there eyebrows and green eyes scanning Da Hood's unknown quarters.

I glanced down and through the smoke spotted the $20.00. We'd be riding together for awhile I surmised.

The next week, Shady Grady a tall pale white guy came over from Basic.

Cesar, my boss came over to my desk, "Listen to Robert, he is very great."

"Yeah I know," replied Shady, "I sat with him before when we were both in basic."

"Okay," the young Haitian man returned to his motivating antics for the rest of the floor. "Let's get some leads…leads…leads-- we need some leads…leads…leads. I know you can do it Tiffany. Just tell them how you feel--and that you need this lead."

Shady remarked to me, "That Cesar's a piece of work," in his Philly, laid back and confident manner.

I plugged in the double headset so he could listen in. My pitch hadn't changed at all from Basic. So I didn't train him as I normally would a newcomer. He'd do fine--an older gentleman in his fifties and fit too. We talked sports for the balance of the afternoon until Shady informed Cesar he'd heard enough and could go it alone on the phone.

The ensuing weeks, I laughed whenever listening to the various pitches on the Burt block; for Burt was Shady's first name. Aside from Burt Grady, Burt Sussman, and me Burt Panta; the Burt block perimeter consisted of Bruno Avi, and Tiffany Jennings, the only black girl in our corner; and we were the only predominantly white block in a black majority on the floor. Some pitches were:

'A very simple Process--may save you some money,' Burt Grady.

'Give us an Opportunity,' the New York bossiness yelped off small, bald, Burt Sussman's booming voice belying his slight frame.

'Why?' Tiffany would whine on in rebuttal to a customer's protest.

And finally directly across from me in his Latin accent when trying to locate the household's absent spouse,

'Are you the wife? The wife? The wife?!' Bruno Avi scattered ever more urgently with any customer's delay to such an inquiry.

My pitch was conventional with the possible exception of the first two words,

'Yes hello?'

This greeting helped on two counts. One on the predictive dialer, the customer would often have said hello to the telephone rep, who wasn't yet plugged into the call perhaps. And two, it sounded friendly to me, like we were already familiar and our conversation was expected to occur; inevitably, a good way to get the lead cooking.

"How did you get the job? I asked Raymond one day at lunch break.

"I was looking in the paper and I saw S FL telemarketers. I remember looking at the words and thought to myself, 'S FL.' That could mean so fucking long," he laughed.

"What do you mean?"

"I mean--it had been so fucking long since I had a steady job. Even before, I went to prison, I did...I did a lot of odd jobs. See, I always tried to follow my plan. Otherwise, if you don't...you become part of somebody else's plan."

I wanted to interject, 'but you are working for some one else now.'

"So fucking long, I thought. How much

longer do I have to listen to this insanity on the phone and around me. A part of my soul dies every time I walk through those doors. I just wanna be a big author--not even big. But just to be doing it and touring and doing the press and the radio for it. So fucking long...I've waited..."

Raymond interrupted, "Let's quit--so fucking long. I want to do this book gig too. I'll tell you the story. You can tape record it. It'll be great. We could tour together. Let's just give our notice."

"How long should we give?" I asked.

"What if they fire us? We both have mortgages--my boat, your kid.

"Come on man! We only have one life. Let's go. Think of it--no more obscenities shouted at us--those incoming calls especially." Ray grabbed a notebook out of my hands and ripped out a sheet of paper.

'Watch...we're audi- so fucking long, one month notice,' as he scribbled,

'So Fucking Long,' with two lines underneath, marking a spot for our signatures. He signed and handed the pen to me to seal our fate.

The blackness of squid and whiteness of timbre beckoned my call.

I thought of all the hoopla, crazy telemarketers I've know in South Florida. The magazine lady who fired me because I pointed out a minor error in her script. 'She does that to everyone,' informed the cute blond as she ran after me to cool my jets.

Then there was the Rockford Files with Crazy Walter with dark glasses in his blue plaid suit; the tall man proclaiming 'Whose the superstar today? Are you the superstar?' he address me once. I shrugged, ashamed to be selling septic tank additives.

And next, Giuseppe, the frizzy haired Armenian, who marveled at my three sales in a row, after murmurings of him wanting to fire me embered among the three or four other people on my shift in the dilapidated warehouse.

Lastly, I remembered the gold coin crooks, who tried to finagle their way onto QVC (home shopping network) television. They offered me a GM position then took it away; probably sensing I wasn't crooked enough to pull wool for long.

The top producer among the telephone

rep producer here proclaimed,

"These doctors and lawyers have people kissing their asses all day long. You gotta shake'em, bully'em. I tell them, 'You've heard me, he shouted from back to a balding man afraid to look at the aggressive former stock broker with a pit-bull build,

'Mr. Jones-- I bet I could take you by the ankles, hang you upside-down and Three Grand would drop out of your pockets.'

He continued, "Usually they laugh at that. If not, I say, and this always breaks them up,

'Come on! After the commission the boss here gets, I barley have enough money for a biggie shake and a biggie fry.' "You gotta be tough."

I never tried this method, as I stated before. My style wasn't to intimidate, but to gently lead them into the sale.

The people at my current job were nice, with the Bible references; I was comfortable with them in the trenches. In light of Ray's signature and my open space, I didn't know what I should do. Should I go back and read one of those Bible passages to tell me where to go. Did Ray Chevrolet have the answer by me signing my name and making my own way?

Ray looked at me, "Come on--lunch is almost over. We've got to either punch in or punch out. Are you going to sign the paper?

"This place always was purgatorial to me, Ray. I too asked myself after almost every one of those damn calls, 'What did I do in another life to deserve this?'"

He broke into a great grin and slapped my back as I bent over to sign my name.

I asked Raymond, "Hey, who would've thought Ray, that the blackness of squid and the whiteness of timbre were the answer for us telemarketers used to speaking for a living?"

He answered, "Like I said to my cell mate once, 'the only way out is through.' "

We clocked out and said to a shocked Scott and Cesar who had their feet kicked up on the desk with the ghetto music blaring.

"So Fucking Long!" in our own singular blast between bass beats.

As the ink dried Ray and I made our escape and figured we'd created our break.

So fucking long.

THE END

10 - Hurricane Warning

The sound trumpeted into my ear, ringing it and trampled up my spine, chilling me to the core.

"Stay Awake!"

What could this mean? That I needed to stay awake all night? I was already tired and had to wake up for Mass at 7:30 for the eight o'clock service.

What would befall me if I didn't? There were no hurricane watches or warnings, though the season forecast for many. We were only in early August.

It perturbed me. I'd been devoted to going to church everyday. And here I was on a Thursday night, attempting to get some shuteye and terrifyingly awake at 2:35 in the a.m. Every day I seemed to get less sleep, awakening earlier each day of the week, starting on Monday. Now a warning that I was to get none, having tossed and turned til one in the morn. The voice was so stern. I couldn't discern as I looked in horror at the turquoise alarm numbers in the middle of the silver speakers of the brash alarm clock, whether the voice was a fallen angel or one from God. What were good angels supposed to sound like? Or bad ones, what did *they* sound like for that matter?

The angel must be from God I surmised. It wouldn't be a trick, not after I'd been praying the rosary religiously right after Mass--before breakfast even!

But what should I do about it? Did the messenger really expect me to stay up all night? And if I did would he repeat the request the following night. Oh, it was too much for my body and soul.

Fast forward a few weeks. I kept up my daily Mass routine. Then word came. A hurricane the size of a small moon forecast for the Florida peninsula. Frances. It took the confirmation name of my ex-fiancee. Holy cow! The main reason I moved down here was her. Frances. The folks at the National Hurricane Center even had the gender right. I felt this as payback, in a negative way.

Nightmares hadn't taunted me in over two years. And suddenly I have an angel with a voice as clear as day and a fiat which seemed like an Eleventh Commandment to me; the fear the missive elicited in me wouldn't stop on following nights.

Fear's a funny thing. Every one in a hurricane warning feels it. But I've learned through my first hurricane experience, that how each individual handles the internal pressures, more so than the external ones is what counts. Isabelle told me 'those with faith stay.' And Maria, my neighbor illuminated 'Where you gonna run to? Just be with the Lord. They taught me that.

They had families. I was envious of that. Easy for them to say. In fact, everyone around me had family, friends, spouses, or at least a child that they could hunker down with before Frances pegged us. I was slated to bunker down alone. I had nothing.

So I tried to flee. In a panic, I called and begged for a flight to anywhere outside of the tropical peninsula, the place where everyone comes to play; but now, we all might have to pay.

This ominous feeling felt like my ex's personal vendetta against me, serving a final misery decree to my sunshine state.

Anyhow, anywhere turned out to be Denver, a two o'clock flight on Friday. The airport in Orlando closed at about noon on Thursday. Fort Lauderdale would close midday on Friday. Would Miami follow suit? If so I'd be stuck in Miami Beach, on the water where the storm surges were expected to be highest.

The current situation was the storm may head north, but it may also make a sharp left turn into Miami. Hurricane Andrew in 1992 taught residents in Homestead of last minute jogs in the hurricane cells to deviate where they may as Andrew initially was predicted to assault the folks awaiting it with trepidation in Fort Lauderdale. Who knew what controlled their frenetic deviations?

Denise from my former employer said in a phone conversation that it figures Hurricane Frances was named after a woman as the storm was stalling in the Bahamas. I couldn't understand why she hadn't rushed to buy shingles or plywood, taking a cavalier approach toward the powerful storm.

By phone she informed me, "'Gilbert did his own thing back in 1988 I remember, a man, in and out; that was a category five in Jamaica. I survived that one so now I'm tired of stressing myself out. I finally said, 'Don't worry Denise.'"

Frances was a four now, but could pick up to a five over the warm Bahamian waters. I would be taking a risk going to the airport. For the news told of nine hour delays for ticket holders. I didn't have a ticket just a reservation that I could cancel within 24 hours; I hadn't even held it with a credit card because I'd cut them up months ago. So obtaining a boarding pass was a longshot. Everything felt like a longshot except the ominous feeling that Frances had drawn a bead on me. I was on part of its track and felt as if I needed to do everything within my power to stay away from its menacing path, (particularly its eye).

I would be taking a calculated risk going to the airport, I thought, as Enrique carried the plywood with me past my living room out now through the sliding glass door to the balcony overlooking the pool. He moved fast. The Brazilian from San Paolo was a perfectionist as he marked the lines twice on the wood before cutting with his circular saw.

"Damn I'm good," he said. He drilled as I held the wood, shielding my eyes.

"How are we going to get down from my balcony up here when we finish boarding this sliding glass door up?" I asked.

"I don't know we could be like Spiderman and swing like on the mast of my sailboat. He pointed to it over his left shoulder as the light breeze blew his brown hair loosely across his forehead. The twenty six foot sailboat with the red mast was docked in front of my small motorboat.

"We could jump into the pool," I suggested with seriousness.

"Oh man, you're crazy."

"We could make it just stand up on here and jump…"

"Come on." He finally stopped laughing. "You see how shallow it is there."

"No. It's five foot in the deep end."

"Shit. You'd never make it."

"What are you talking about? It's only a five foot broad jump."

"I can't jump five feet."

"Sure you can. Well, I bet it's only three feet with the trajectory, us being up here on the second floor."

"Now way."

"Maybe we should ask some one for a ladder."

Enrique examined me with incredulity. He then peered around my balcony's right side wall barrier to as my neighbor Joaquin something in Spanish.

"Did he have one?"

"One what?"

"A ladder." I gave him a what else look.

"I didn't ask him." He examined my perturbed face and peered quickly leaning over the gold barred rail.

"Hey do you have a ladder Joaquin?"

Enrique turned to me, "He doesn't have one." He examined the dimensions of the board and the panes of glass carefully.

Several holes were drilled and all went well until I complained about the dust a few times. I could see he grew tired of my grumblings, which were more than I care to recall and he admonished me twice for my impatience. He was a handyman supreme whose services were demanded by many in our condo complex. And when the neighbors weren't barging into my place bombarding him with request to help them prepare for the monster cane, the very moment these distractions subceased and I began to rejoice, inevitably his cell phone would ring and it'd be a request for a boating assistance call, as he once had worked in a boatyard. He had two boats himself he had to take care of today as well as my boat. We needed to take the motor off mine. And then we were to finish his apartment in time to assist his friends upstairs on the fifth floor with more plywood.

"I'm going upstairs. I need to eat something."

I paused. The silence aggravated him I could sense.

"Is that okay?"

"Sure."

Hours passed. I grew anxious. I should've been making phone calls to other acquaintances like Anna, my old girlfriend's older sister. But I couldn't work up the nerve. I knew they were to stay with a friend in Coral Springs. I couldn't intrude. Besides they may call me yet to ask for my whereabouts during the hurricane. Denise invited me to stay with her. But she didn't have plywood for Home Depot had sold out. I'd went the day before. 'Lucky I got canned on Monday,' I told the pale, big boned girl who was a nurse. We'd both purchased our wood and awaited our respective rides outside but outside of the chaos of immigrants scrambling around tying down wood on vans, cars, or loading it into trucks. I leaned on the pushcart out of the sun and wedged into the open oversized garage area where the air conditioner breathed on us. We had a sweet spot amidst the preambling of storm players.

She told me she was upset because her employer insisted she work the day before the storm was to hit and now had to rush to put up the plywood.

'That's a great attitude,' she remarked about my buoyed spirits in light of unemployment and a hazardous storm. She meant it. I suddenly beamed. It was a good attitude. I beamed, proud of myself. Why couldn't my friends or Enrique have been there to hear it? I stressed for no good reason. I said goodbye to the girl as we loaded Enrique's truck.

In Enrique's bedroom, I asked Julia, Enrique's wife where they were going, as he changed drill bits as fast as a surgeon in an emergency room striving to save his son. I found it a little odd he took such painstaking care in boarding up his place. The inside resembled Beirut, clutter galore. How did they ever find anything? A hurricane may actually organize the displaced papers and furniture.

"We're going to Iowa," Enrique answered for Julia.

"Flying or driving?"

"Driving, he blustered brusquely.

"My aunt and uncle are up there," Julia elaborated. "We were going to…"

"Visit them for Christmas anyways," interrupted Enrique, "but it looks like we're going earlier, a vacation, unplanned," he laughed. "We can't stay here with the baby."

Julia rocked little Antonio in the cluttered bedroom.

"Let me show you the mural in Antonio's room," Enrique said excitedly.

"Wow. Who did that?" I asked.

"I did," Enrique proudly sowed me the seagulls, dolphin, sun and palm trees.

It was quite tranquil; and big and cool--very Miami yet appropriate for a child.

In spite of my genuine enthusiasm and as neat as it was, I found it difficult to get him to stop talking and move back to the window we'd been boarding up by his workbench, which covered the entire length of the wall.

He leaned on the workbench and turned to retrieve another drill bit.

Ah good. Back to work, I thought.

Extending my short arms, I held the board up. My right shoulder ached from holding up wood for two days straight as we'd actually begun the night before.

Julia chimed in, "We're going to paint this workbench a mahogany finish. It's going to look good when it's done."

"You kidding? It's going to be great!" Enrique enthused.

Early the next morning, I drove home from church and listened to Enrique on my cell phone.

"I'm over on Key Biscayne helping my friend with his boat. But don't worry I'm on my way."

I felt somewhat confident we'd have enough time to finish, or finish at least my unit; I wasn't sure about the rest of the docket, Enrique's friends et al. The reason for my optimism was due to reports that Frances was slowing. We needed to do the other side of the sliding glass door and pull the motor off my boat too-plenty of time even if he came at noon. His wife said he changed his mind that they were going to Tampa instead of Iowa which took me by surprise in light of the fact that the cone field seen on the television weather reports drew a line straight through to Tampa after it decked southeast Florida; all the models showed this. And Enrique had seemed so certain last night of going to Iowa even going so far as to invite me to tag along to the corn field's with them. Part of me wanted to accompany them to Iowa, but my next choice was to stay with the rest of the residents here. But Enrique regarded me as insane when I laid out, "Why don't you just stay here?"

"No way not with the baby," he retorted.

I had to call my parents by nightfall to let them know the locale I planned to ride out the storm. Earlier in the morning after church I spoke with Isabelle and she admitted that she hadn't decided what to do either. Isabelle lived in a rental and the landlord wouldn't board the place up. She asked him if I could store my boat there in the yard next to another similar size boat, which didn't pan out she informed me that morning.

Instead my boat would risk its physical characteristics as we humans would ours. I was concerned that Enrique said we'd throw the anchor from my boat, which was tied tight with whips by my allotted portion of the seawall, to the middle of the canal because there's no automatic drainage; it runs off the battery and one has to manually flick the toggle switch on the panel as well knobs there for navigation lights and aerator pump; it was necessary Enrique informed me that the battery must also be removed.

I asked him, "What if we get flood rains from the storm?"

"Then it may sink." He studied my frown. "Yeah, that's okay. We'd get it out."

"How?"

"Its shallow here. I've done it before. Don't worry."

'Don't worry' became a common command for me to adhere to during these precarious hurricane preparations, by my various phone companions and neighbors alike. Thelma Eisenburg upstairs told me, "It's a strong building."

But she's biased I thought, since she was the chairwoman on the condo committee for so many years.

"What about flooding? My boat, my car?"

She replied in her old lady voice, "We didn't have a drop after Andrew in '92. And we have a very good drainage system here. Aha--Hmm."

I was skeptical, but did recall that after some intense rain last summer, the drainage was indeed extremely fast. But this was a hurricane--a Cat 4 Hurricane!

"Enrique is going to Iowa," I informed her.

"Iowa?" He's crazy," the diminutive but fiery Jewish woman crackled.

After we continued standing watching the weatherman, I blurted, "Who's staying with you?"

On the outside chance that it was no one and I could at least have the option of staying at one more residence; for Thelma possessed the Trump of all condo's, equipped with a state of the art automatic heavy duty shutters. Possibly the only downside in her fortress was the fact that it was one floor higher than I and objects tended to move faster at greater heights, even in the span of twenty to thirty feet. But above all, if welcome, at lest I could ride out the storm with another human being.

"Neil," she answered, followed by her usual tag, "Aahem-Hmm."

Shit. It'd be tough enough to persuade Thelma to allow me to stay with her, never mind her son Neil, who I'd only met in the elevator coolly a couple times.

"Okay, I gotta run to see to whom Enrique is lost to now," I excused myself.

I called Isabelle in the middle of the commotion--the drilling the dust sweeping into my eyes from all angles. When she picked up, her voice calmed me.

"Are you going to Denver?"

"No. I decided against it. That reminds me, I'll need to call to cancel."

"Good, then maybe if me and my daughter decide not to stay in Hialeah we can come over. We can die together."

Silence.

"That was a joke," she finished.

"Yeah-Ha...ha" I weakly laughed.

"Do you think you'll go to Hialeah for the hurricane? Your friend has the aluminum shutters, right?"

"Yes, but...I don't know--my friend's place. Sometimes I don't know if she really wants me there because there's lots of clutter she tells me."

I wanted to interrupt and say, it's no problem--that I'd sleep in it, against it, on it, even under any rummage that existed...inside. Plus, can you imagine the major clutter a category 5 hurricane could compile?

"Anyways, maybe you will call your other friend...you told me...Anna in Coral Springs, isn't it?"

"Yes."

"Try her."

"Okay, but that's north and the storm track has it moving that way. I think Hialeah is safer. I definitely would like to go south."

"All right. Well, let me check. I think it is a little funny, no? A man. If I bring a man with my daughter. You guys can take us anywhere. But the other way around people get..."

"Funny." I felt awful aiding in my own

un-vitation.

"Yes. But I will try," she attempted to stay upbeat.

As soon as I set down the receiver, I dialed Anna while flipping through the five various worn phone books, two Dade county, two Broward, and...damn, no Monroe county for the Keys. I desired to book a reservation at the Keys, which for a change was not in the direct path of a major Florida cane.

"Hello. Hello." Anna had picked up while I sprawled on the floor sitting, skimmed the Hotel section in the Miami Dade phone book in case a Keys Hotel was cross-referenced. I greeted her prior to her possible premature hang-up as her impatience tended to wane as quickly as mine.

"What doing?" my Chinese friend who was like an older sister inquired.

"Desperately trying to find a place to stay. How about you?"

"I go to Coral Springs." It was only through familiarity with her painstaking problems with r's and l's that I could decipher the otherwise butchered pronunciation of the small city west of Pompano; for she tended to say it differently each time, obscuring clarity even further; but again I picked up on it.

"Sherry's place?"

"No her apartment with her roommate is too crowded. You remember Paula...her house."

"Good. They have shutters?"

"No," she said matter of fact.

"Plywood?"

"No. I don't think so."

"Well, I must tell you, I don't think you should go up north. It's very dangerous without shutters or plywood. The objects fly through the air and can crash through the window easily. Then once the wind whips inside, you can forget it. It wrecks everything in its path."

Though I'd never witnessed the phenomena firsthand, I imparted some of Enrique's knowledge to the uninformed Chinese friend.

She protested, "But Jeffrey, he wants to go. You know...my son--go play with Jennifer, Paula's daughter. He hasn't played with in long time. He looking forward to it."

"There will be plenty of time to play later. You need to be safe. I think you should go to a shelter. North Miami Beach High School is the nearest one. I can give you directions."

"No, no that's okay. Oooh, Sherry call me know! I talka you tonight...Bye bye," her voice trailed off as well as my hopes to sway her. It occurred to me I was acting as a surrogate parent to Jeffrey or an estranged husband to Anna. When I lost Sherry, I lost what little influence I once possessed in that family too. I felt the aloneness seep into my being. I was always alone, but the likely tragedy and crises that the imminent hurricane promised, thrust that singleness of fact mercilessly and violently at me, yet further and possibly most disturbingly, flaunting it in the neighbors I witnessed in communion with one another.

My body tightened more with each passing thought. The massage I'd had at the Bal Harbor less than a week ago seemed a distant memory and a false cure to the ailment of aloneness. The past couple nights no hypnologic niceties of a prelude to sleep existed. It was anxiety through and through. And now it was a roller coater of horrible twists and strains intensifying as the hurricane's eye did. Yet I fathomed frightfully...It's eye could certainly stay open longer than mine despite my messenger's strong warning.

"Enrique is helping another friend with a boat," Julia updated me through her screen door.

"That's all right. He'll be back in the afternoon, right?"

"Absolutely," she reassured.

I felt better. Julia was solid. I decided to go downstairs and try to relax.

"Have him call me when he returns home," I told her.

Unable to unwind, I kept staring at the one piece of plywood. If he didn't come back by two or three o'clock then we'd really be under the gun. I needed to take my mind off that. I felt like exercising. I maintained a yoga pose or two but not for long then glanced at the phone book on the coffee table that I'd made reservations with United Airlines. I stared at the plywood pleading for its twin. Could I rely on this handyman? He's good. I know that. But he has the tendency to be absent. Absenteeism is fine for teachers or employment, but not when some one's life, manly mine is on the line. I can trust him. He told me and his wife are good Catholics like myself. However, a flight out of Miami was tempting. I'd be gone Friday afternoon and returning Monday afternoon. I tried to envision flying over the Rockies. It sounded like a winter paradise. I didn't know why I got on the horn so quick.

I hesitated before calling. Holding the receiver, I realized, 'I'm playing with my life':

'You only get one,' the words of the black woman I spoke to on the telephone from the Red Cross rang in my ears, (but not as loud as the angel's).

Screw it, 'I'll roll the dice.' I dialed United, read my confirmation number and then asked while their representative evidently pulled it up on the computer screen slowly.

"Is the flight still going? I saw on T.V. that most airlines have cancelled all their flights." My fate seemed to wait on her reply.

"No. That one is still slated to go...as of now."

"Hmm...I...I...I guess I'll cancel.' The words came out and immediately I felt as if I'd broke ground on my own plot.

Where the fuck is Enrique? I walked downstairs in the dense humid air, muttering aloud. I searched for his red truck, nowhere to be found. I took the elevator to see Julia. They lived on the west side of the Elevator whereas Thelma resided on the east.

Enrique's door opened. "Oh, hi Shezzy," Julia warmly greeted.

"Hi. Where's Enrique?"

She was still smiling. That was good.

"He's stuck in Miami. Unfortunately, his battery went dead. Can you believe it?"

"I thought he was in Biscayne Bay on a boat."

"He was. He parked downtown and got stuck after a few traffic lights. He's upset. I need to pick him up now. I will have him call you right away. Don't worry. There are four other guys that are going to help you two. So it'll be quick."

Okay. At least that delimitative phrase rang gleefully, placating me as I headed for the short elevator ride downward with my eyes fixed toward the canned salmon color apartment floor light, 2. I stepped out of the elevator, my neighbor Minnie, Joaquin's wife, asked me for confirmation,

"You're staying?"

"I don't know I'm still thinking of going with Enrique and Julia to Iowa, or maybe Hialeah, or up to Fort Lauderdale. Where do you think is the safest place?"

She shrugged, lit her cigarette, took a puff and hung over the balcony viewing the men and women across the street boarding up. "All this," she waved her cigarette as if dismissing the busy bodies around her, "is unnecessary. The hurricane is probably going to do nothing. It'll go away--like this smoke," she laughed heartily.

I turned around and noticed Minnie's woodless front window, "Aren't you guys going to at least board up?"

"What for? I'm telling you it's nothing. This happens every year. I've been here a long time. It's only because the last eight years have been quiet that the people now become nervous. You'll see."

"I don't know. It would be easier if I was with some one during this hurricane."

"Just be with the Lord. That's all you need."

Easy for her to say. She had her husband. And I was as undecided as ever as I watched the television and they targeted our area even more. It hadn't veered and showed no signs according to the weatherman.

When the men finished boarding my place up and Enrique and friends finally helped me lift my motor and battery depositing them in the middle of my living room, and the confusion surrounding these frantic finalizations ceased I thanked Enrique.

It seemed unspoken that I'd decided to ride out the storm here alone. Though I secretly wished he would ask me to go to Iowa with him and his family. Minutes later, around 9:30p.m., while Enrique showered, I raced after Julia who was packing the car. I gave her a check.

"Thanks, but I don't think Enrique will cash it."

"Stay safe," I said.

"You too."

And I began the remainder of my hurricane preparations, filling water in pans, putting candles on plates in strategic locations. Oh yeah, the closet--that could be the final spot of repose if the wind broke in.

I opened my Bible and like Minnie said…waited with the Lord.

THE END

11 - A Dollar's Value

"Stanley Carey is in the house."

On such a greeting, I always turned to wave to my boss from my center stage position, an open desk on the main West Gate entrance of the track. Jay Conrad's loud salutation always made me feel welcome. He was followed by Howard, the other man in the two-man marketing department at the Greyhound Track. They passed through the vestibule and turned into the glass office door, which locked upon shutting. This locking was the first of several changes to discourage employees and customers alike.

Some days he'd come out to shoot the shit with me; others, he'd stay back there all day and if he worked nights, all night until one of his escorts would show up, he'd bring her out to show her off.

"This is Stanley Carey--I hired him. He's the whole show here." The girl would smile as Jay introduced her and she usually didn't speak much English, but her beauty superseded the track's surroundings. That much was obvious. I wondered if they slept with him. None were serious or so I thought for there were no pictures of them when I retrieved my allotment of Player Club cards that I could conveniently access in the executive offices. I was the only non-exec to have the privilege of entering the offices.

For I enjoyed helping myself to coffee, which to my chagrin often drew the ire of Vince Marlowe, the Director of Security Operations for the track. He gave me the evil eye except when Jay was around. Though he was never quite ever lukewarm to my presence. He ordered me around even though he wasn't my boss and I tensed for fear of running into him in the hallway or even avoiding his raised eyes from behind his desk off the hallway first door on the right; I'd creep by his desk. A slick Pat Riley/Bob Deniro 'do distinguished gentlemen in his seventies; a perfect caricature for his job. But everyone fit their prospective molds here. I realized you'd need thick skin to last here. Being put through the paces by Joe was a tune-up for the real show outside.

Security infiltrated the floors. Uniformed jackets everywhere. Maybe that's why it seemed Joe possessed supreme power. Hell, Jay Conrad even feared him though he'd help Joe because of his age; but Jay would help everyone.

"What can I do for you?" was his motto.

Though I never asked, he too the time to explain the psychology of the gambler to me. I wished I could remember it. It's interesting side chatter. But let's take a look at those circumstances that make up the cast

---

Larry was talking to Jenny the black security guard.

"I need to buy a car."

"New?" asked Jenny.

"No--used. A used one is all I need."

"Come on Larry. You've got money. I see you lending out loads of it here to these down-on-their-luck losers."

He laughed shirkily--his old man's humble pie laugh.

"You're so sweet Larry. I don't know why you be so generous to these guys.

They're just trying to yoohz..-..."

Larry turned suddenly as if he'd heard a million times the potentially lethal phrase lasered at his sole defection; and not wanting to hear the plain truth he said, "Where's the ATM?" He began walking away from her, the wrong way.

Jenny called loudly, "You know where it is. Where ya going? It's right over here, behind the advertisement board. Same place it's been for years, Larry."

"Years," he repeated. "That's what I've got behind me. I'll tell you. Eighty two years old. I've seen a lot. I fought in World War II. Those were though years. I had all my friends die--my brother too. I stayed with my sister for quite a few years after that, up in Jersey. Then I came down here."

"You been in that car since you came here." Jenny pointed to his beat up Pontiac with the window broken and the top cover torn.

"No no. That's my second, no third car, third car since I came to Florida. I buy'em used, all used. I learned the value of a dollar-- I tell you that. A long time ago I learned the value of a dollar."

He said it as though that pearl, a lost art

evaded Jenny's generation. "Why don't you get some dollars then and buy me an ice cream bar Larry?" his comment prompted her to so quip. "No I'm only kidding. I shouldn't ask. Everyone asks you for money. Jenny felt some shame.

"I'm going to get a hot dog. You know what they say, 'the only good dog is a hot dog!' Ha ha."

She laughed with him too. Her bright teeth shone through her éclair, deep chocolate Haitian skin.

"You're going to miss the daily double," she added.

"I only bet through the fifth race. That's all I usually do up to the fifth or sixth race. Then I just hang out. I learned the value of a dollar. Some of these guys they go broke in here--not too smart. But not me. I learned…that…I tell you."

"What's my pin number? Hey. Can you show me which way this card goes? I keep forgetting. I'm doing something wrong."

I started my shift. Jenny and I didn't speak much the first couple weeks of my employment. I kept busy going up and down the stairs, scouting, trying to solicit strangers. I walked by a teller who barked,

"What the fuck--I gave you the right change asshole!" He replied violently to a customer.

"Check the ticket again, shit-for brains."

"Screw you, jerk off. I did twice."

"I'm talking to your manager. I'll have you're job."

"Go ahead. Good luck in finding him."

I couldn't believe the decibel level of the exchange. How on earth could I function here at a dog track. I was a corporate prep boy from Dallas. I was going to have to approach these gloom-filled characters in the cigarette haze of the first floor, a wide open space interspersed with televisions both side of each of the several wooden pillars shooting to the ceiling dividing the track and floor in two.

After the second week, Jay was pleased. He told me to keep up the good work. On a double I could sign up maybe over a dozen people. Even Vince seemed satisfied with the numbers. This was a relief to me because I got wind that he had wanted to hire another security guard instead of creating my brand new position.

"Now Stanley, remember," Jay addressed me fatherly as my eyes followed the wrestling posters around the walls of his office and the picture directly behind his desk, Jay standing proudly with ex-football great Lawrence Taylor, "if anyone asks you how to do the job, don't tell them. Don't let them see the computer. You have access to all the bettors' records. The Player Tracking system is top secret. And please don't tell the security guards that it's an easy job; otherwise, Vince will try to fire you. Keep it low key as always. I'm not worried about you. But I'm only telling you once. All right?"

"Sure Jay, got it. No problem."

"Good now take these."

"Now I can't. Why don't you give them to some one else or you go!"

"No no. It's a reward. I know someone like you is overqualified for this work so this'll help make up for it."

They were luxury box seats to the Panthers vs. Dallas Stars game.

Jay was always doing stuff like that for me.

Around the second week of work, I met T-Lo and Singing Al. Singing Al called her that because she was Latin and resembled J-Lo minus the ass. Al could sing. T-Lo couldn't. We'd ask him for requests. Mine were outlandish for his age bracket--he was about eighty. I'd write the words to 'Emotional Rescue' and Al would sing Mick's lyrics in an old classic Sinatra pitch, but it actually sounded good. I had to laugh hysterically and more than T-Lo, though it cracked a smile in her too.

"Did you go to church?" Al asked T-Lo.

"No Al. I've got too many things to do than to go…three jobs. It's not easy."

"Three. Well, why don't you redo your schedule so you can go to church on Sunday."

"I'm too tired on Sunday."

"Well Saturday night then."

"I'm here."

They always tried to figure her schedule out.

"What numbers do you want to play?"

"Three-Eight. They're my lucky numbers."

"Okay--I'll place it. Hold my spot." Then to me, "Young fella…" He suddenly recalled my name, "you go to church Stanley?"

"Yes."

"See. He's a nice fellow. You oughta follow his example. But his problem, see is he tries to get everyone to sign up to gamble. Not everyone has a problem in gambling institutions, but some do. They lose everything. T-Lo, I think you're answer is to quit this job, just drive the bar and train your dogs. That's the ticket--so you can go to church. This is an evil place. An evil empire-- built on greed. Greed--it's...it's... it's just terrible; his old voice creaked and his green eyes verily twinkled with welling sadness.

"Al, how can I quit. I'm so in debt to my sister and…"

"Well, I think the people here are all going to hell…"

"Al! What are you talking about?"

"You--you have to look at that. Maybe if you go to church…"

"It'd help," I chimed in.

They seemed surprised that I'd spoken.

"See," Al boasted, "even Stanley agrees. But he's going around…" He then addressed me.

"I see you trying to sneak around and convince everyone to gamble--with those cards of yours." There he pointed to the stack of six or seven that I typically carried in my palm with me; the rest remained in my front pockets.

"Stanley--he'll be on top of all the people in here, going to hell. I bet on that," and he laughed, bobbing his head, shaking feebly yet sweetly with his Irish grin. His brown sports coat, open as he sat on the stool next to T-Lo.

I turned my head back to my computer screen to pretend I had important business, though there were no prospects in sight to reel in.

"See Al, you upset him. Not everyone is bad you know."

"Well...I know that. The three-eight, right?" He walked away dragging his feet under his light beige sport coat. His image and motion reminded me of a bent broom sweeping debris, losing old crumpled tickets discarded on the floor.

As I rode the escalator up to the pool room his comments kept warbling, sing-songing peskily in my ear.

Months passed by. I signed up hundreds

upon hundreds of potential playing patrons. The winter was fun. Tourists joined regulars so Larry and Al took more of a backseat. Or perhaps there was less time to recognize them.

Sometimes Al would sing loud enough above the din or Larry would talk about how the only good dog was a hot dog. Life at the track went on. Dogs sometimes ran the wrong way on the track, or flipped over the guardrail. T-Lo would ask Al for the summary, "Which race was that in?"

One night when Larry was by the ATM machine and warily I whispered to T-Lo, "Larry showed me his balance once--sixty thousand."

"You shouldn't show people that Larry," T-Lo admonished him. Some one's going to take advantage of you."

"Don't worry about me," he huffed. "I learned the value of a dollar. I know when to quit. I draw the line with certain people."

"Why don't you get a card Larry?"

"No. I can't keep track of that."

"But you get money back right?" T-Lo asked.

"Yeah, you get money or food or store discounts. We comp you for your bets. The amount bet counts as points. I can give you the application for the Player Club and sign you up now?"

"Are you a player Larry?" Jenny, who had just punched in smiled as she saw Larry look over the application.

"No, Not me."

"What about you Al?" plead T-Lo You're here all the time too. You guys should have the card." She then turned to me and said lowly, "See, I'm helping you solicit." Her sexy Latin wink and slow drawled out pronunciation on solicit made me blush.

'I don't need that. I heard the tellers don't know how to use them to credit the bettors. I like to be in and out fast so I can watch the races," said Al.

There was some truth in that. I'd given up having Jay enforce and make clear that the tellers needed to be nice to the players with the cards. Hell, they paid my salary.

A man with black hair and blackened teeth breathed vodka on me as he said,"

"Excuse me sir. I'm having a problem with this card--in the Dog House Restaurant they told me to see you."

I looked up and noticed his Cowboys hat and exclaimed, "You a Cowboys fan?"

He held up his hand as if he wanted to talk more about the card. But he said,

"Theyyy'rre the best," then held in a belch.

"I forgot your last name."

"Why do you need that?"

"To look you up in the system."

"Oh. Can you take the card?"

"Oh yeah. There's a number on the back."

"Larry--Hey Larry. Excuse me. I'll do this later," He grabbed the card quickly out of my hand before I could look up his betting points.

The man begged Larry, "I need a twenty."

"Yeah, all right. All right. Here you go."

The man looked down on Larry's gray head. It reminded me of my Uncle Joe's kind Italian face; and his build was also a replica, tiny but scrappy and witty too, always at the ready with a joke. It was like he was reincarnated here. I recalled a picture taken in The Dallas Maverik of Uncle Joe, standing on the track as it was in the process of being torn down. He loved life his daughter said at the memorial service. I felt warm watching him; generously giving his dough away freely. But this feeling gave way to twinges of resentment toward the Cowboy-capped rugged, hockey-mouthed sloth towering over him waiting for his latest beggar's beckon to the old man's ATM balance.

"Why did you give him that money?"

Jenny had punched in, and strolled over, overhearing and replied for old Larry,

"He always be doing that--giving money to these nuts. What's the nut to sane ratio in here T-Lo?"

"No one can tell. Once you walk through these doors all sane people become a little nutso in here."

"Hm-hmm. Just a matter of time. You'll see Stanley," Jenny forewarned.

A sunny day I spotted Howard outside as he occasionally took breaks on the near bench. Howard told me to sit down. I knew something was wrong.

"Aaagh--Jay died last night."

"What? No."

"I went over to his house and he was just

laying there. I kept having that image stuck in my mind."

"A heart attack," I suggested.

"Jay lived life...I tried to tell him to quit eating so much and partying and..."

"I'm sorry Howard,"

"Yeah. There's a funeral at 2pm today."

In the two hour interim, I spoke to Larry.

"I've got go to my bosses funeral," I droned.

"Which boss?"

"Jay Conrad."

"Jay. Oh, oh-no. He was young wasn't he?"

"Fifty two or fifty three I think."

"That's young. I'm eighty two."

"Do you think I...I bought him a present--something doesn't seem right about Howard's explanation of how he died."

"How did he die? Heart attack?"

"I--that's what he said but it didn't sound convincing or right to me...I--you know?"

"What else would it be?"

"I think he had a final fantasy living in the fast lane. Maybe an escort depicted in a book I bought for him...I think he tried to relive that scene, vicariously through the novel."

"You gotta be careful what you spend your dollars on. I learned the value of a dollar."

I answered Larry, "Right so. I wish I hadn't bought that book.

THE END

Printed in the United States
58277LVS00001B/10-57